ROSSHALDE

Rosshalde

HERMANN HESSE

TRANSLATED BY
RALPH MANHEIM

JONATHAN CAPE
THIRTY BEDFORD SQUARE LONDON

First published 1914 in Germany under the title *Rosshalde*
Copyright S. Fischer Verlag 1914
Copyright renewed 1941 by Hermann Hesse, from *Gesammelte Schriften*
Copyright 1956 by Suhrkamp Verlag, Berlin und Frankfurt/M
This translation first published in Great Britain 1971
Translation © 1970 by Farrar, Straus and Giroux, Inc.

Jonathan Cape Ltd, 30 Bedford Square, London WC1

ISBN 0 224 00502 2

Printed in Great Britain by
Lowe & Brydone (Printers) Ltd, London
Bound by James Burn & Co. Ltd, Esher, Surrey

ROSSHALDE

Chapter One

TEN YEARS AGO when Johann Veraguth bought
Rosshalde and moved in, it was an abandoned old
manor with overgrown garden paths, moss-covered
benches, cracked stone steps, and a tangled, neglected
park. The only buildings on the property, which measured about eight acres, were the fine, slightly run-down
manor house with its stable, and in the park a small
temple-like summer house, its door hanging askew on
bent hinges and its walls, formerly hung with blue silk,
covered with moss and mold.

Immediately after purchasing the house, the new
owner had torn down the decrepit temple, leaving only
the ten old stone steps that descended from its thresh-
old to the edge of the fish pond. In its place Veraguth's
studio was built. Here for seven years he had painted
and spent most of his time, but he had lived at the
manor house until the increasing dissension in his
family had led him to send his elder son away to
boarding school, to leave the manor house to his wife
and servants, and for his own use to add two rooms to
the studio, where he had been living as a bachelor ever

since. It was a pity about the fine manor house; Frau Veraguth and the seven-year-old Pierre used only the upper floor; she received visitors and guests but never very many of them, so that a number of the rooms were empty all year round.

Little Pierre was the darling of both parents, the only bond between father and mother; not only did he maintain a certain contact between the manor and the studio, in a sense he was the sole lord and master of Rosshalde. Herr Veraguth's domain was his studio, the lake shore, and the former game preserve, while his wife reigned over the house, the lawn, and the lime and chestnut groves. Seldom did either of them visit the other's territory, except at mealtimes, when the painter usually went to the manor house. Little Pierre alone did not recognize, indeed he was hardly aware of, this division of life and territories. He came and went as freely in the old house as in the new, he was as much at home in his father's studio and library as in the hallway and picture gallery of the manor house, or in his mother's rooms; he was lord over the strawberries in the chestnut grove, the flowers in the lime grove, the fish in the lake, the bathhouse and the gondola. In his dealings with his mother's maids and Robert, his father's servant, he felt himself to be both master and protégé; in the eyes of his mother's visitors and guests he was the son of the lady of the house, and in the eyes of the gentlemen who sometimes came to Papa's studio and spoke French, he was the painter's son. Paintings and photographs of the boy hung in his father's bedroom and in the mother's rooms in the old house with their light-colored wallpaper. Pierre was very well off, better off indeed than children whose parents live in harmony; his upbringing was not regulated by any program, and when, as sometimes happened, he was in trouble in his mother's domain, the lakeside territory offered him a secure refuge.

He had gone to bed long before, and at eleven o'clock the last window in the manor house had darkened. Long after midnight, Johann Veraguth returned alone from town, where he had spent the evening with friends at a tavern. As he strode through the balmy, cloudy, early summer night, the atmosphere of wine and smoke, of red-faced laughter and outrageous jokes had fallen away from him; consciously breathing in the warm, damp, slightly tense night air as he walked alertly down the road between the dark fields of already well-grown grain, he approached Rosshalde with its massed treetops silent against the pale night sky.

Passing the entrance to the estate, he glanced at the manor house; its noble, luminous façade shone alluringly against the black darkness of the trees, and for a few minutes he gazed at the lovely scene with the pleasure and strangeness of a passing traveler; then he

(3

HERMANN HESSE

continued on for a few hundred paces along the high
hedge to the place where he had made an opening from
which a secret path led through the woods to the studio.
His senses keenly awake, the small powerful man
walked through the somber, overgrown park toward his
house; the dark treetops surmounting the lake seemed
to open, a great sphere of dull-gray sky came into view,
and suddenly the house was before him.

The little lake lay almost black in the total silence,
the feeble light lay on the water like an infinitely thin
membrane or a layer of fine dust. Veraguth looked at
his watch, it was almost one. He opened a side door
leading into his living room. Here he lighted a candle
and quickly undressed; naked, he left the house and
slowly descended the broad flat stone steps into the
water, which for an instant glittered in soft little rings
before his knees. He plunged, swam a little way out into
the lake, suddenly felt the weariness of an evening
spent in an unaccustomed way, turned back, and
entered the house dripping. He threw a bathrobe over
his shoulders, smoothed the water from his close-
cropped hair, and barefoot climbed the few steps leading to his studio, an enormous, almost empty room,
where with a few impatient movements he quickly
turned on all the electric lights.

He hurried to an easel bearing a small canvas he had
been working on in the last few days. Bending forward

4)

with his hands on his knees, he stood before the picture
and stared at the surface, whose fresh colors reflected
the harsh light. So he remained for two or three minutes, staring in silence until the entire picture, down to
the last brush stroke, came alive in his eyes; in the last
few years he had become accustomed on nights before
working days to take no other image to bed and sleep
with him than that of the painting he was working on.
He put out the lights, picked up the candle, and went to
his bedroom, on the door to which hung a small slate.
He picked up the chalk, wrote in bold letters: "Wake at
seven, coffee at nine," closed the door behind him, and
went to bed. He lay for a short while motionless with
his eyes open, compelling the picture to take form on
his retina. Saturated with it, he closed his clear gray
eyes, heaved a gentle sigh, and soon fell asleep.

In the morning Robert awakened him at the ap-
pointed hour; he rose at once, washed in cold running
water, slipped into a faded suit of coarse gray linen,
and went to the studio; the servant had pulled up the
heavy shutters. On a small table stood a dish of fruit, a
carafe of water, and a piece of rye bread. He thoughtfully picked up the bread and bit into it while standing
at the easel looking at his picture. Pacing back and
forth, he took a few bites of bread, fished a few cherries
out of the glass bowl, and noticed that some letters and
newspapers had been laid on the table but ignored

(5

them. A moment later he was sitting on his camp chair looking tensely at his work.

The little picture in horizontal format represented an early morning scene which the painter had witnessed and done several sketches of in the course of a trip. He had stopped at a little country inn on the upper Rhine. The friend he had come to see was nowhere to be found. He had spent an unpleasant rainy evening in the smoky taproom and a bad night in a damp bedroom smelling of whitewash and mold. Before sunrise, he had waked hot and disgruntled from a light sleep. Finding the house door still locked, he had climbed out of the taproom window, untied a boat on the nearby bank of the Rhine, and rowed out into the sluggish, barely dawning river. From the far shore, just as he was about to turn back, he saw a fisherman rowing toward him. Its dark outline bathed in the cold, faintly quivering light of the milky rainy daybreak, the skiff seemed unnaturally large. Instantly captivated by the scene and by the strange light, he had pulled in his oars while the man came closer, stopped at a floating marker, and raised a fish trap from the cool water. Two broad, dull-silvery fishes appeared, glistened wet for a moment over the gray river, and then fell with a smack into the fisherman's boat. Bidding the man to wait, Veraguth had fetched a rudimentary paintbox, and had done a small water-color sketch. He had spent the day in the village, sketching and reading; the next morning he had painted again in the open, and had then resumed his travels. Since then he had turned the picture over and over in his mind, suffering torments until it took shape. Now he had been working on it for days and it was almost finished.

As a rule he painted in the bright sun or in the warm, broken light of the park or forest, so that the flowing silvery coolness of the picture had given him a good deal of trouble. But it had shown him a new tone, he had found a satisfactory solution the day before, and now he felt that this was good, unusual work, something more than a commendable likeness, that in it a moment out of nature's mysterious flow burst through the glassy surface, giving an intimation of the wild, full breath of reality.

The painter studied the picture with attentive eyes and weighed the tones on his palette, which, having lost nearly all its reds and yellows, bore little resemblance to his usual palette. The water and the air were finished, the surface was bathed in a chill, unfriendly light, the bushes and stakes on the shore floated like shadows in the moist, livid half light; the crude skiff in the water was disembodied and unreal, the fisherman's face was speechless and undefined, only his hand reaching out calmly for the fish was alive with uncompromising reality. One of the fishes sprang glistening over the gunwale of the boat; the other lay flat and still, its round open mouth and rigid frightened eye full of creature suffering. The whole was cold and almost cruelly sad, but irreproachably quiet, free from symbolism except of the simple kind without which there can be no work of art, which permits us not only to feel the oppressive incomprehensibility of all nature but also to love it with a kind of sweet astonishment.

When the painter had been sitting at his work for about two hours, the servant knocked and in response to his master's absent call brought breakfast in. He quietly set down the pitchers, cup, and plate, moved up a chair, waited awhile in silence, and then announced diffidently: "Breakfast is served, Herr Veraguth."

"Coming," said the painter, rubbing out with his thumb a brush stroke he had just made on the tail of the leaping fish. "Is there hot water?"

He washed his hands and sat down to his coffee.

"You can stuff a pipe for me, Robert," he said cheerfully. "The little one without a cover, it must be in the bedroom."

The servant went. Veraguth drank the strong coffee with fervor, and the faint suggestion of dizziness and exhaustion, which had been coming over him lately after strenuous effort, lifted like morning mist.

He took the pipe from the servant, let him light it, and greedily breathed in the aromatic smoke, which intensified and refined the effect of the coffee. He pointed at his picture and said: "You went fishing as a boy, Robert, I believe?"

"Yes, Herr Veraguth."

"Take a look at that fish, not the one in the air, the other with its mouth open. Is the mouth right?"

"It's right," said Robert distrustfully. "But you know better than I do," he added in a tone of reproach, as though sensing mockery in the question.

"No, my friend, that is not true. It's only in early youth, up to the age of thirteen or fourteen, that a man perceives things in all their sharpness and freshness; all the rest of his life he feeds on that experience. I had nothing to do with fish as a boy, that's why I ask. So tell me, is the nose right?"

"It's good, it's perfectly right," said Robert, flattered.

Veraguth had stood up again and was examining his palette. Robert looked at him. He was familiar with this concentration that came into his master's eyes and gave them an almost glassy look; he knew that he, the coffee, and their little conversation were vanishing from Veraguth's mind and that if he were to address him in a few minutes, the painter would wake as though from a deep sleep. But that was dangerous. As Robert was clearing the table, he saw the mail lying there untouched.

"Herr Veraguth," he said softly.

The painter was still accessible. He cast a hostile glance over his shoulder, very much in the manner of an exhausted man spoken to when on the point of falling asleep.

"Your mail."

With that, Robert left the room. Veraguth nervously squeezed a blob of cobalt blue on his palette, tossed the tube on the little lead-sheathed painting table, and began to mix his colors. But then he felt troubled by the servant's reminder. Irritably he put the palette down and picked up the letters.

The usual business correspondence, an invitation to contribute to a group exhibition, a request from a newspaper for biographical information, a bill—but then a thrill of joy passed over him as he caught sight of a handwriting he knew well; he picked up the letter and delightedly read his own name and every word of the address, taking pleasure in the strong character of the free, impetuous pen strokes. He tried to read the postmark. The stamp was Italian, it could only be Naples or Genoa. So his friend was already in Europe, not far away, and could be expected in a few days.

With emotion he opened the letter and looked with satisfaction at the rigorous order of the short straight lines. If his memory did not deceive him, these infrequent letters from his friend abroad were the only pure joy he had experienced in the last five or six years, except for his work and the hours spent with little Pierre. And now once again, in the midst of his joyous expectancy, a vague, unpleasant feeling of shame came over him at the thought of his impoverished, loveless life. Slowly he read:

Naples, 2 June, night

Dear Johann,

As usual, a mouthful of Chianti with greasy spaghetti, and the shouting of the peddlers outside the wine shop, are the first signs of the European culture to which I am once again returning. Here in Naples nothing has changed in five years, much less than in Singapore or Shanghai; I take this as a good sign and am encouraged to hope that I shall find everything in good shape at home as well. The day after tomorrow we shall be in Genoa, where my nephew is meeting me. We shall visit our relatives together. I expect no great effusions of sympathy in that quarter because to be perfectly frank I have not earned ten talers in the last four years. I figure on four, five days for the most pressing family obligations, then business in Holland, say another five, six days, so I ought to be with you on about the sixteenth. You will receive a wire. I should like to stay with you for at least ten days or a fortnight, and interfere with your work. You have become dreadfully famous, and if what you used to say some twenty years ago about success and celebrities was even halfway true, you must be quite gaga by now. I mean to buy some paintings from you and my foregoing lamenta-

B

tions about the state of business are a maneuver to hold your prices down.

We are growing older, Johann. This was my twelfth trip across the Red Sea and for the first time I suffered from the heat. 115 in the shade.

Think of it, old man, only two weeks! It will cost you a bottle of Moselle. It's been more than four years.

A letter will reach me from the ninth to the fourteenth in Antwerp, Hôtel de l'Europe. If you have any pictures showing on my itinerary, let me know!

Yours,
Otto

In high good humor, he reread the short letter with its sturdy, erect letters and temperamental punctuation, took a calendar from the drawer of the little desk in the corner, and wagged his head with satisfaction as he looked at it. Up to the middle of the month, more than twenty of his paintings would be on exhibit in Brussels. That was a good thing. It meant that his friend, whose sharp eye he rather feared and from whom he would not be able to conceal the devastation of his life in the last few years, would at least have a good impression of him, an impression he could take pride in. That would make everything easier. He saw Otto with his somewhat rough-hewn transoceanic elegance striding through the Brussels gallery, looking at his paintings, his best paintings, and for a moment he was thoroughly glad he had sent them to the show, though only a few were still for sale. And he immediately wrote a note to Antwerp.

"He still remembers everything," he thought gratefully. "He's right, the last time we stuck almost entirely to Moselle, and one night we really drank."

On reflection, he concluded that there was sure to be no Moselle left in the cellar, which he himself rarely visited, and decided to order a few cases that very day.

Then he sat down again to his work, but felt distracted and uneasy and was unable to regain the pure concentration in which good ideas come unsummoned. He put his brushes in a glass, pocketed his friend's letter, and sauntered irresolutely into the open. The mirror of the lake glittered up at him, a cloudless summer day had risen, and the sun-drenched park resounded with the voices of many birds.

He looked at his watch. It was time for Pierre's morning lessons to be over. He strolled aimlessly through the park, looked absently down the brown, sun-mottled paths, listened in the direction of the house, walked past Pierre's playground with its swing and sand piles. At length he approached the kitchen garden and looked with momentary interest up into the high crowns of the horse-chestnut trees with their shadow-deep masses of leaves and last joyous-bright candles. The buzzing of the bees came and went in soft waves as they swarmed round the many half-open rosebuds in the garden hedge, and through the dark foliage the merry little turret clock in the manor house could be heard striking. The number of strokes was wrong, and Veraguth thought again of Pierre, whose proudest ambition it was, later, when he was bigger, to repair the ancient clockwork.

Then he heard, from the other side of the hedge, voices and steps which in the sunny air of the garden blended softly with the buzzing of the bees and the cries of the birds, with the lazy-blowing fragrance of the carnation border and of the bean blossoms. It was his wife with Pierre; he stood still and listened attentively.

"They're not ripe yet, you will have to wait a few days more," he heard the mother say.

The boy's reply was a twittering laugh. For a fragile, fleeting moment the peaceful green garden and the soft resonance of this childlike conversation, muffled by the breeze, seemed in the expectant summer stillness to come to Veraguth from the distant garden of his own childhood. He stepped up to the hedge and peered through the leaves into the garden, where his wife in a morning dress stood on the sunny path, holding a pair of flower shears in her hand and on her arm a delicate brown basket. She was hardly twenty paces from the hedge.

The painter watched her for a moment. The tall

figure was bending over the flowers; her grave, disillusioned face was entirely shaded by a large, limp straw hat.

"What are those flowers called?" asked Pierre. The light played over his brown hair, his bare legs stood thin and sunburnt in the bright glow, and when he bent down, his loose-fitting blouse revealed the white skin of his back below his deeply tanned neck.

"Carnations," said the mother.

"Oh, I know that," said Pierre. "I want to know what the bees say to them. They must have a name in the bee language too!"

"Of course, but we can't know it, only the bees know. Perhaps they call them honey flowers."

Pierre thought it over.

"That's no good," he finally decided. "They find just as much honey in clover or nasturtiums; they can't have the same name for all the flowers."

The boy was attentively watching a bee as it flew around the calyx of a carnation, stopped in mid-air with buzzing wings, and then hungrily penetrated the rosy hollow.

"Honey flowers!" he said contemptuously, and fell silent. He had discovered long ago that the prettiest and most interesting things are the very ones that cannot be known or explained.

Veraguth stood behind the hedge and listened; he

(15

observed the calm earnest face of his wife and the lovely, prematurely fragile face of his darling, and his heart turned to stone at the thought of the summers when his first son was still such a child. He had lost him, and his mother as well. But this child he would not lose, no no. Like a thief behind his hedge he would spy on him, he would lure him and win him, and if this boy should also turn away from him, he had no desire to live.

Soundlessly he moved off over the grassy path and withdrew beneath the trees.

Loafing is not for me, he thought irritably, and hardened himself. He went back to his painting and indeed, overcoming his disinclination and surrendering to old habit, he recaptured the industrious tension which tolerates no digressions and concentrates all our energies on the work in hand.

He was expected for lunch at the manor house, and at the approach of noon he dressed carefully. Shaved, brushed, and clad in a blue summer suit, he looked perhaps not younger but fresher and more resilient than in his shabby studio clothes. He reached for his straw hat and was about to open the door when it opened toward him and Pierre came in.

"How are you, Pierre? Was your teacher nice?"

"Oh yes, only he's so boring. When he tells a story it's not for the pleasure, it's just another lesson, and the end is always that good children must do like this or like that. —Have you been painting, Papa?"

"Yes, working on those fishes. It's almost finished, you may see it tomorrow."

He took the boy's hand and went out with him. Nothing in the world so soothed him or touched the submerged kindness and tenderness in him as to walk beside the boy, to adjust his pace to his short steps, and to feel the child's light trusting hand in his own.

As they left the park and started across the meadow beneath the spindly drooping birches, the boy looked around and asked: "Papa, are butterflies afraid of you?"

"Why? I don't think so. One sat down on my finger a little while ago."

"Yes, but there aren't any here now. Sometimes when I go over to see you by myself and I come this way, there are always lots and lots of butterflies on the path, and they're called blues, I know that, and they know me and they like me, they always fly around right close to me. Is it possible to feed butterflies?"

"Indeed it is, we must try it very soon. You put a drop of honey on your hand and hold it out very quietly until the butterflies come and drink it."

"Wonderful, Papa, we'll try. Won't you tell Mama she has to give me a little honey? Then she'll know I really need it and it's not just foolishness."

Pierre ran ahead through the open gate and the broad hallway; blinded by the sunlight, his father was still looking for the hatrack in the half light, and groping for the dining-room door, long after the boy was inside, pressing his plea on his mother.

The painter entered and held out his hand to his wife. She was somewhat taller than he, strong and fit, but without youth, and though she had ceased to love her husband she still regarded the loss of his affection as a sadly incomprehensible and undeserved misfortune.

"We can eat right away," she said in her even voice. "Pierre, go and wash your hands."

"I have news," said the painter, handing her his friend's letter. "Otto is coming soon, for a long stay I hope. You don't mind?"

"Herr Burkhardt can have the two downstairs rooms, then no one will disturb him and he will be able to go in and out as he pleases."

"Yes, that will be fine."

Hesitantly, she said: "I thought he wasn't coming until much later."

"He set out sooner than he had expected. I knew nothing myself until today. Well, so much the better."

"Now he will be here at the same time as Albert."

At the mention of his son's name, Veraguth's face lost its faint glow of pleasure and his voice grew cold.

"Albert?" he exclaimed irritably. "He was supposed to go to the Tyrol with his friend."

"I didn't want to tell you any sooner than necessary. His friend was invited to visit relatives and gave up the walking trip. Albert will be coming as soon as his vacation starts."

"And stay here the whole time?"

"I believe so. I could travel with him for a few weeks, but that would be inconvenient for you."

"Why? Pierre would come to live with me in the studio."

"Please don't begin that again. You know I can't leave Pierre here alone."

The painter grew angry. "Alone!" he cried bitterly. "He's not alone when he's with me."

"I can't leave him here and I don't wish to. There's no point in arguing about it any more."

"I see. You don't wish to."

He fell silent, for Pierre had come back, and they sat down to table. The boy sat between his estranged parents, both of whom served him and entertained him as he was used to having them do. His father tried to prolong the meal as much as possible, because after lunch the boy stayed with his mother and it was doubtful whether he would come to the studio again that day.

Chapter Two

R OBERT WAS IN THE SMALL WASHROOM next to the
studio, busy washing a palette and a bundle of
brushes. Little Pierre appeared in the open doorway. He
stopped still and watched.

"That's messy work," he said after a while. "Painting
is all very well, but I'd never want to be a painter."

"Maybe you ought to think it over," said Robert.
"With such a famous painter for a father."

"No," said the boy decisively, "it's not for me. Always
filthy and always such a strong smell of paint. I like to
smell just a bit of it, on a new picture, for instance,
when it's hanging in a room and there's only a tiny
smell of paint; but in the studio it's too much, I couldn't
stand it, it would give me a headache."

The servant looked at the child searchingly. He
ought really to have given this spoiled child a good
lecture long ago, there was much to find fault with. But
when Pierre was there in front of him and he looked
into his face, it was impossible. His face was so fresh
and pretty and grave; everything about him seemed to

be just right, and just this streak of the blasé, this arrogance or precocity, was strangely becoming to him.

"What would you actually like to be, my boy?" Robert asked with some severity.

Pierre looked down and reflected. "Oh, I really don't want to be anything special, you know. I only wish I were through with school. In the summer I'd just like to wear all white clothes, white shoes too, and never have the tiniest spot on them."

"I see, I see," said Robert reproachfully. "That's what you say now. But when you were out with us the other day, all of a sudden your white clothes were full of cherry stains and grass stains, and you'd lost your hat altogether. Do you remember?"

Pierre froze. He closed his eyes except for a small slit and glared through his long lashes.

"Mama gave me a big scolding for that," he said slowly, "and I don't believe she gave you orders to bring it up again and torture me with it."

Robert took a conciliatory attitude. "So you would always like to wear white clothes and never get them dirty?"

"No, sometimes I would. You just don't understand! Of course I'd want to lie around in the grass sometimes, or in the hay, or jump over puddles or climb a tree. That's as plain as day. But when I've finished running wild, I don't want to be scolded. I just want to go quietly to my room and put on clean fresh clothes, and then everything will be all right again. —Do you know, Robert, I really don't see any point in scolding."

"That *is* convenient. How so?"

"Well, look: if you've done something that isn't right, you know it and you're ashamed. If somebody scolds me, I'm much less ashamed. And sometimes they scold you when you haven't done anything at all, just because you weren't there when they called, or because Mama is in a bad humor."

Robert laughed. "You've just got to average it up. Think of all the wicked things you must do that nobody sees and nobody scolds you for."

Pierre gave no reply. It was always the same. Whenever he let himself be drawn into a discussion with a grownup about something that was really important to him, it ended in disappointment or even humiliation.

"I'd like to see the picture again," he said in a tone which suddenly put him at a distance from the servant. Robert might equally have taken his words as a command or a request. "Come on, let me in for a second."

Robert obeyed. He opened the studio door, admitted Pierre, and followed him, for he had strict orders not to leave anyone alone in the studio.

Veraguth's new painting, in a temporary gilt frame,

had been placed on the easel in the middle of the large room, turned toward the light. Pierre planted himself in front of it. Robert stood behind him.

"Do you like it, Robert?"

"Of course I like it. I'd be a fool not to."

Pierre blinked at the picture.

"I believe," he said thoughtfully, "you could show me a whole pile of pictures and I'd know right off if one of them was by Papa. That's why I like his pictures, because I feel that Papa made them. But, to tell you the truth, I only half like them."

"Don't talk nonsense," said Robert, horrified, with a reproachful look at the boy, who, quite unruffled, stood blinking at the picture.

"You see," he said. "There are some old paintings over there in the house that I like a lot better. When I grow up, I want to have pictures like that. Mountains, for instance, when the sun is setting and everything is all red and gold, or nice-looking children and ladies and flowers. Such things are really a lot nicer than an old fisherman like this who hasn't even got a real face, and a nasty black boat. Don't you agree?"

At heart Robert agreed perfectly; he was surprised and indeed delighted at the boy's frankness. But he would not admit it.

"You're too young to understand such things," he said curtly. "Come now, I have to lock up."

(23

At that moment a chugging and grinding was heard from the direction of the manor house.

"Oh, a car!" cried Pierre joyfully, and ran out under the chestnut trees, taking forbidden shortcuts across the lawns and jumping over the flower borders. Breathless, he reached the gravel driveway in front of the house just in time to see his father and an unknown gentleman alighting from the car.

"Pierre!" cried his father, and caught him in his arms. "Here is a friend you don't know any more. Give him your hand and ask him where he's come from."

The boy looked the stranger straight in the eye. He gave the man his hand and looked into a ruddy-brown face and bright laughing gray eyes.

"Where have you come from?" he asked obediently.

The stranger picked him up in his arms. "You're getting too heavy for me, son," he said with a cheery sigh, and put him down again. "Where do I come from? From Genoa and before that from Suez, and before that from Aden, and before that, from . . ."

"Oh, from India, I know, I know! And you're Uncle Otto Burkhardt. Have you brought me a tiger, or coconuts?"

"The tiger ran away, but you can have coconuts and shells and Chinese picture albums."

They entered the house and Veraguth led his friend, who was a good bit taller than himself, up the stairs, putting his arm affectionately round his shoulder. Upstairs in the hallway they were met by the lady of the house. With restrained but sincere cordiality she welcomed the guest, whose hale cheerful face reminded her of happy times in years gone by. He held her hand in his for a moment and looked into her face.

"You haven't aged any, Frau Veraguth," he complimented her. "You've held up better than Johann."

"And you haven't changed at all," she said amiably.

He laughed. "Oh, the façade is still in good shape, but I've given up dancing. Besides, it wasn't getting me anywhere, I'm still a bachelor."

"This time, I hope, you've come to Europe to look for a wife."

"No, Frau Veraguth, it's too late for that. And I wouldn't want to spoil my stay in Europe. I have relatives, you know, and I'm gradually developing into an inheritance uncle. I wouldn't dare turn up at home with a wife."

Coffee had been served in Frau Veraguth's room. They drank coffee and liqueurs and chatted for an hour about ocean voyages, rubber plantations, and Chinese porcelain. At first the painter was quiet and slightly depressed. He had not set foot in this room for months. But it all went off smoothly and with Otto's presence a lighter, more cheerful, more childlike atmosphere seemed to have come into the house.

"I believe my wife would like to rest awhile," said the painter at length. "Come, Otto, I'll show you your rooms."

They took their leave and went to the guest rooms. Veraguth had prepared the two rooms for his friend, attending to everything himself. He had arranged the furniture and thought of everything from the pictures on the wall to the books in the bookcase. Over the bed hung a faded old photograph, a touchingly comical class picture dating back to the seventies. It struck the guest's eye, and he went closer to look at it.

"Good Lord!" he cried in amazement. "There we are, all sixteen of us! What a touching thought! I hadn't seen that in twenty years!"

Veraguth smiled. "Yes, I thought it would amuse you. I hope you find everything you need. Do you want to unpack now?"

Burkhardt sat down squarely on a large steamer trunk with copper corners and looked about him with satisfaction. "This is perfect. And where are your quarters? Next door? Or upstairs?"

The painter played with the handle of a leather bag.

"No," he said offhandedly. "I live over in the studio now. I've added to it."

"You must show me that later. But . . . do you sleep over there too?"

ROSSHALDE

Veraguth dropped the bag and turned around. "Yes, I sleep over there too."

His friend fell into a thoughtful silence. Then he reached into the bag and took out a bundle of keys which he began to jangle. "Should we do a little unpacking? You could go and get the boy, he'll enjoy it."

Veraguth went out and soon returned with Pierre.

"You have beautiful luggage, Uncle Otto, I've been looking at it. And so many tags. I've read a few. One of them says Penang. What's Penang?"

"It's a city in Malaya where I go sometimes. Come, you can open this."

He gave the child a flat, intricate key and bade him unlock a suitcase. It sprang open, and the very first thing to meet the eye was an inverted flat basket of bright-colored Malay wickerwork. They turned it over and removed the wrapping; inside, padded with paper and rags, there were lovely, strangely shaped shells such as are offered for sale in exotic seaports.

The shells were a present for Pierre, who was too happy to speak, and after the shells came an ebony elephant and a Chinese toy with grotesque movable wooden figures, and finally a roll of garish-colored Chinese prints, full of gods, devils, kings, warriors, and dragons.

While the painter joined the boy in admiring his

c

presents, Burkhardt unpacked the leather bag and put slippers, underwear, brushes, and so on, in their places. Then he went back to his friends.

"Well," he said cheerily, "that's enough work for today. Now to pleasure. Could we take a look at the studio?"

Pierre looked up, and again, just as when the car had driven in, his father's animated face, grown youthful with pleasure, filled him with surprise.

"You're so gay, Papa," he said approvingly.

"Yes indeed," Veraguth nodded.

But his friend asked: "Isn't he usually so gay?"

Pierre looked from one to the other with embarrassment.

"I don't know," he said hesitantly. But then he laughed again and spoke up: "No, you've never been so cheerful."

He ran off with his basket of shells. Otto Burkhardt took his friend's arm and they went out. Veraguth led him through the park to the studio.

"Yes," Burkhardt observed at once, "I can see the change. I must say it looks very nice. When did you do it?"

"About three years ago. The studio has been enlarged too."

Burkhardt looked around. "The lake is marvelous. Let's go for a little swim this evening. You have a beautiful place here, Johann. But now I want to see the studio. Have you any new paintings here?"

"Not very many. But there's one I want you to see, I only finished it the day before yesterday. I think it's good."

Veraguth opened the doors. The high studio was festively neat, the floor freshly scrubbed, and everything in its place. The new painting stood all by itself in the middle of the room. They stood facing it in silence. The heavy damp-cold atmosphere of the dismal rainy dawn contrasted with the clear light and hot, sundrenched air that came in through the doors.

They viewed the work for a long while.

"Is this the last thing you've painted?"

"Yes. It needs a different frame, otherwise there's nothing more to be done. Do you like it?"

The friends looked searchingly into each other's eyes. The taller and stouter Burkhardt with his ruddy face and warm eyes full of the enjoyment of life stood like a large child before the painter, whose face seemed sharp and severe in its setting of prematurely gray hair.

"It's perhaps your best picture," said the guest slowly. "I saw the ones in Brussels and the two in Paris. I'd never have expected it, but you've gone still further ahead in these few years."

"I'm glad to hear you say that. I think so too. I've worked pretty hard. Sometimes I think I was nothing but a dilettante before. I was late in learning how to work properly, but now I've mastered it. I probably won't go any further. I can't do anything better than this."

"I understand. Well, you've become very famous, I've even heard people talking about you on our old East Asia steamers, and I was very proud. How does it feel to be famous? Does it make you happy?"

"Happy? No, I wouldn't say that. It seems right. There are perhaps two, three, four painters who amount to more and have more to offer than I. I've never counted myself among the really great; what the journalists say is nonsense. I have a right to be taken seriously, and since I am, I'm satisfied. All the rest is newspaper glory or a question of money."

"I suppose so. But what do you mean by the really great?"

"The kings and princes. My kind can get to be a general or minister, that's as far as he can go. The most we can do is to work hard and take nature as seriously as possible. The kings are nature's brothers and friends, they play with her, they create where we can only imitate. But of course there aren't very many kings, not one in a hundred years."

They walked back and forth in the studio. Casting about for words, the painter stared at the floor, his friend walked beside him and tried to read his sallow lean face.

At the door to the adjoining room, Otto stopped. "How about showing me your living quarters?" he said. "And let's have a cigar."

Veraguth opened the door. They passed through the living room and looked into the other little rooms. Burkhardt lighted a cigar. He went into his friend's bedroom, saw his bed, and carefully examined the alcoves littered with painting equipment and smoking accessories. The general effect was almost of poverty; the home of an ascetic, hard-working bachelor.

"So you've settled over here," he said dryly. But he could see and feel everything that had happened in the last few years. He observed with satisfaction the objects suggestive of sports, gymnastics, horseback riding, and noted with concern the absence of any sign of well-being, creature comfort, or enjoyment of leisure.

Then they went back to the painting. So this was how these pictures, hung in the places of honor in galleries all over the world and sold at high prices, were made; they were made in rooms that knew only work and self-denial, where one could find nothing festive, nothing useless, no cherished baubles or bric-a-brac, no fragrance of wine or flowers, no memory of women.

Two photographs were nailed over the narrow bed,

one of little Pierre and one of Otto Burkhardt. Burkhardt remembered it well. A poor snapshot, it showed
him in a tropical helmet with the veranda of his Indian
bungalow behind him; just below chest level, the picture disintegrated into mystical streamers where light
had fallen on the plate.

"The studio is beautiful. And what a hard worker
you've become! Give me your hand, old friend, it's
wonderful to see you again. But now I'm tired, let me
disappear for an hour. Will you call for me later on, for
a swim or a walk? Fine. No, I don't need anything. I'll
be all right in an hour. Until then."

He sauntered off slowly under the trees and Veraguth looked after him, observing how his stature and
his gait and every fold of his clothing breathed self-
assurance and serene enjoyment of life.

Burkhardt went into the house, but passed his own
rooms, climbed the stairs, and knocked on Frau Veraguth's door.

"Am I disturbing you, or may I keep you company for
a little while?"

She admitted him with a smile; he found the brief
unpracticed smile on her grave face strangely helpless.

"It's magnificent here in Rosshalde. I've already been
in the park and down at the lake. And how Pierre is
thriving! He's so attractive, he almost makes me feel
sorry I'm a bachelor."

"He is nice-looking, isn't he? Do you think he takes after my husband?"

"Yes, a little. Well, actually, more than a little. I didn't know Johann at that age, but I remember pretty well how he looked when he was eleven or twelve. —Incidentally, he seems a bit tired. What? No, I was speaking of Johann. Has he been working very hard recently?"

Frau Veraguth looked into his face; she felt that he was sounding her out.

"I believe so," she said coolly. "He seldom speaks of his work."

"What is he working on now? Landscapes?"

"He often paints in the park, usually with models. Have you seen any of his pictures?"

"Yes, in Brussels."

"Is he showing in Brussels?"

"Oh yes, quite a number of pictures. I've brought the catalogue. You see, I should like to buy one of them and I'd be glad to know what you think of it."

He held out the catalogue and pointed to a small reproduction. She looked at the picture, leafed through the catalogue, and gave it back.

"I'm afraid I can't help you, Mr. Burkhardt, I've never seen the picture. I believe he painted it last fall in the Pyrenees and has never had it here."

After a pause she changed the subject. "You've given

Pierre a lot of presents, that was very kind of you. Thank you."

"Oh, little things. But you must permit me to give you something from Asia too. You don't mind? I have some bits of cloth I'd like to show you, you must choose what you like."

By turning her polite sparring into a gracious, whimsical little battle of words, he managed to overcome her reserve and put her in a good humor. He went down to his treasure trove and returned with an armload of Indian fabrics. He spread out Malay batiks and hand-woven goods and threw laces and silks over the backs of the chairs, meanwhile telling her where he had found one piece or another, how he had haggled over it and purchased it for a song. The room became a colorful little bazaar. He asked her opinion, hung strips of lace over her arms, explained how it was made, and made her spread out the finest pieces, examine them, feel them, praise them, and finally keep them.

"No," she laughed when he had done. "I'm reducing you to beggary. I can't possibly keep all this."

"Don't worry," he laughed in return. "I've just planted another six thousand rubber trees, I'll soon be a regular nabob."

When Veraguth came for him, he found the two of them chatting as merrily as could be. He was amazed to see how loquacious his wife had become, tried in vain to join in the conversation, and admired the presents rather clumsily.

"Forget it," said his friend, "that's the ladies' department. Let's go for a swim!"

He drew his friend out into the open.

"Really, your wife has hardly aged at all since I saw her last. She was in high good humor just now. You all seem to be doing all right. But what about your elder son? What's he up to?"

The painter shrugged his shoulders and frowned. "You'll see him, he'll be here any day now. I wrote you about him."

And suddenly he stopped still, bent toward his friend, looked him straight in the eye, and said softly, "You'll see everything, Otto. I don't feel the need of talking about it. You'll see. —We really ought to be gay while you're here. Let's go down to the lake. I want to have a swimming race with you, like when we were boys."

"Good idea," said Burkhardt, who did not seem to notice Johann's uneasiness. "And you'll win, old man, which wasn't always the case. I'm ashamed to say so, but I've really developed a paunch."

It was late afternoon. The whole lake lay in the shadow, a light wind played in the treetops, and across the narrow blue island of sky which the park left open over the water flew light violet clouds, all of the same shape and kind, in a brotherly row, thin and elongated like willow leaves. The two men stood outside the little bathhouse hidden in the bushes; the lock refused to open.

"Never mind," said Veraguth. "It's rusty. We never use the bathhouse."

He began to undress and Burkhardt followed suit. When they were on the shore ready to swim, testing the quiet shadowy water with their toes, a sweet breath of happiness from remote boyhood days came over both of them at once; they stood for a minute or two in antici- pation of the delicious chill, and the radiant green valley of childhood summers unfolded gently in their hearts. Unaccustomed to the tender emotion, they stood half embarrassed and silent, dipping their feet into the water and watching the semicircles that fled over the brownish-green mirror.

Then Burkhardt stepped quickly into the water.

"Ah, it's good," he sighed voluptuously. "You know, we can both still bear looking at; except for my paunch, we are still two fine strapping lads."

He rowed with the palm of his hands, shook himself, and plunged.

"You don't know how good you have it," he said enviously. "The loveliest river runs through my planta- tion, and if you stretch out your leg you'll never see it again. It's full of beastly crocodiles. And now full steam

ahead, for the Rosshalde cup. We'll swim to the steps
over there and back again. Are you ready? One . . .
two . . . three!"

Both with laughing faces, they started off at a moderate pace, but the air of the garden of youth was still
upon them, and in a moment they began to race in
earnest; their faces grew tense, their eyes flashed, and
their arms glistened as they swung them far out of the
water. They reached the steps together and together
they pushed off. They started back, and now the painter
pressed ahead with powerful strokes, took the lead, and
reached the finish a little before his friend.

Breathing heavily, they stood up in the water, rubbed
their eyes, and laughed together in silent pleasure. It
seemed to both of them that they had only just now
become old friends again, that the slight strangeness
and estrangement which had inevitably come between
them was just beginning to disappear.

When they had dressed, they sat side by side with
refreshed faces and a sense of lightness on the stone
steps leading down to the lake. They looked across the
dark water which lost itself in the blackish-brown twilight of the overhung cove across the lake, ate fat, light-
red cherries which the servant had given them in a
brown paper bag, and looked on with lightened hearts
as the evening deepened, until the declining sun shone
horizontally through the tree trunks and golden flames

were kindled on the glassy wings of the dragonflies. And they chatted without pause or reflection for a good hour about their school days, about their teachers and fellow students, and what had become of this one or that one.

"Good Lord," said Otto Burkhardt in his fresh, serene voice, "it's been a long time! Does anyone know what has become of Meta Heilemann?"

"Ah, Meta Heilemann!" Veraguth broke in eagerly. "Wasn't she a lovely girl? My portfolios were full of her portraits that I drew on my blotters during classes. I never did get her hair quite right. Do you remember, she wore it in two thick coils over her ears."

"Haven't you had any news of her?"

"No. The first time I came back from Paris, she was engaged to a lawyer. I met her on the street with her brother, and I remember how furious I was with myself because I couldn't help blushing and in spite of my mustache and my Paris sophistication I felt like an idiotic little schoolboy. —If only she hadn't been called Meta. I never could bear that name."

Burkhardt wagged his round head dreamily.

"You weren't in love enough, Johann. I thought Meta was wonderful, she could have been called Eulalia for all I cared, I'd have gone through fire for a glance out of her eyes."

"Oh, I was in love enough. One day on the way back

from our five o'clock free period—I was purposely late, all alone and without a thought for anything in the world but Meta, knowing I'd be punished and not caring—there she was, coming toward me, near the round wall. She was arm in arm with a girl friend. Suddenly I couldn't help thinking how it would be if she were arm in arm with me instead of that silly goose. She was so close to me my head began to swim and I had to stop awhile and lean against the wall. When I finally got back, the gate was closed tight; I had to ring and they gave me an hour's detention."

Burkhardt smiled and remembered how at several of their rare meetings they had reminisced about Meta. As boys they had gone to the greatest lengths to conceal their love from each other, and it was only years later that they had occasionally lifted the veil and exchanged their little experiences. Yet even today neither of them had told the whole story. Otto Burkhardt recalled how for months he had kept and worshipped one of Meta's gloves, which he had found or actually stolen, an episode still unknown to his friend. He considered unburdening himself of the story now, but in the end he smiled slyly and said nothing, taking pleasure in keeping this last little memory to himself.

Chapter Three

BURKHARDT WAS SITTING COMFORTABLY leaning back in a wicker chair, his large panama hat on the back of his head, reading a magazine and smoking in the sun-splattered arbor at the west side of the studio; nearby sat Veraguth on a little camp chair, with his easel in front of him. The figure of the reading man was sketched in, the large color masses were in place, now he was working on the face, and the whole picture exulted in bright, weightless, sun-saturated, yet moderate tones. The air was spiced with oil paint and cigar smoke, birds hidden in the foliage uttered their thin, muffled, noonday cries and sang in sleepy dreamy conversational tones. Pierre was on the ground, huddled over a large map, describing thoughtful journeys with his frail forefinger.

"Don't fall asleep!" shouted the painter.

Burkhardt blinked at him, smiled, and shook his head. "Where are you now, Pierre?" he asked the boy.

"Wait, I've got to read it," Pierre answered eagerly, and spelled out a name on his map. "In Lu—Luce—in Lucerne. There's a lake or an ocean. Is it bigger than our lake, Uncle Burkhardt?"

"Much bigger. Twenty times bigger. You must go there some day."

"Oh, yes. When I have a car, I'll go to Vienna and Lucerne and the North Sea and India, where your house is. But will you be at home?"

"Certainly, Pierre. I'm always at home when guests come. Then we'll go and see my monkey, his name is Pendek, he has no tail but he has snow-white side whiskers, and then we'll take guns and go out on the river in a boat and shoot a crocodile."

Pierre's slender torso rocked back and forth with pleasure. Uncle Burkhardt went on talking about his plantation in the Malayan jungle, and he spoke so delightfully and so long that in the end the boy wearied, was unable to follow, and absently resumed his journey over the map, but his father listened all the more attentively to his friend, who spoke with an air of indolent well-being of working and hunting, of excursions on horseback and in boats, of lovely weightless villages built of bamboo, of monkeys, herons, eagles, and butterflies, offering such seductive glimpses of his quiet, secluded life in the tropical forest that the painter had the impression of peering through a slit into a radiant, multicolored paradise. He heard of great silent rivers in the jungle, of wildernesses full of tree-high ferns, of broad plains where the lalang grass stood as high as a man; he heard of colored evenings on the seashore facing coral islands and blue volcanoes, of wild raging cloudbursts and flaming storms, of dreamy meditative evenings spent on the broad shaded verandas of white plantation houses as hot days sank into dusk, of tumultuous Chinese city streets, and of Malays resting at nightfall beside the shallow stony pond before the mosque.

Once again, as several times before, Veraguth visited his friend's distant home in his imagination, quite unaware that his unspoken yearning responded to Burkhardt's intentions. What bewitched him with images and roused his longing was not only the glitter of tropical seas and archipelagoes, or the color play of half-naked primitive peoples. More than that, it was the remoteness and quietness of a world where his sufferings and cares, his struggles and privations would pale, where his mind would cast off its hundred little burdens and a new atmosphere, pure and free from guilt and suffering, would envelop him.

The afternoon passed, the shadows shifted. Pierre had run away long before, Burkhardt had gradually fallen silent and dozed off, but the painting was almost finished. The painter closed his tired eyes for a moment, let his hands fall, and with almost painful delight breathed in the deep sunny silence of the hour, his friend's presence, his own appeased weariness after successful work, and the letdown of his overstrained nerves. Along with the frenzy of unstinting activity, he had long found his deepest, most comforting pleasure in these gentle moments of weary relaxation, comparable to the restful vegetative twilight states between sleep and waking.

Rising quietly for fear of waking Burkhardt, he carried his canvas carefully to the studio. There he removed his linen painting jacket, washed his hands, and bathed his slightly strained eyes in cold water. A few minutes later he came out again, glanced for a moment inquiringly at his sleeping guest's face, and then awakened him with the old familiar whistle which they had adopted twenty-five years before as their secret signal and sign of recognition.

"If you've had enough sleep, old man," he said cheerily, "you might tell me a little more about India, I could only half listen while I was working. You were saying something about photographs; have you got them here, could we look at them?"

"We certainly could; come along."

For some days Burkhardt had been looking forward to this moment. It had long been his wish to lure Veraguth to East Asia and keep him there with him for a while. It seemed to him that this was the last chance, and he had prepared for it methodically. As the two men sat in Burkhardt's room talking about India in the evening light, he produced more and more albums and

D

packets of photographs from his trunk. The painter was overjoyed and surprised that there should be so many of them; Burkhardt kept very calm and seemed to attach no great importance to the photographs, but in secret he was eagerly awaiting a reaction.

"What beautiful pictures!" Veraguth exclaimed in delight. "Did you take them all yourself?"

"Some of them," Burkhardt said tonelessly. "Some were taken by friends of mine out there. I just wanted to give you an idea of what the place looks like."

He said this as though in passing and with an air of indifference set the photographs down in piles. Veraguth was far from suspecting how painstakingly he had put this collection together. He had had first a young English photographer from Singapore, then a Japanese from Bangkok staying with him for weeks, and in the course of many expeditions from the sea to the depths of the jungle they had sought out and photographed everything that seemed in any way beautiful or worthy of interest; and then the pictures had been developed and printed with the utmost care. They were Burkhardt's bait, and he looked on with intense excitement as his friend bit and sank his teeth into it. He showed him pictures of houses, streets, villages, and temples, of fantastic Batu caves near Kuala Lumpur, and of the jagged, wildly beautiful limestone and marble mountains near Ipoh, and when Veraguth asked if there were no pictures of natives, he dug out photographs of Malays, Chinese, Tamils, Arabs, and Javanese, naked athletic harbor coolies, wizened old fishermen, hunters, peasants, weavers, merchants, beautiful women with gold ornaments, dark naked groups of children, fishermen with nets, earringed Sakai playing the nose flute, and Javanese dancing girls bristling with silver baubles. He had photographs showing palms of every kind, lush broad-leafed pisang trees, patches of rain forest traversed by thousandfold creepers, sacred temple groves and turtle ponds, water buffalo in rice paddies, tame elephants at work and wild elephants playing in the water and stretching their trumpeting trunks heavenward.

The painter picked up photograph after photograph. Some he thrust aside after a brief glance, some he placed side by side for comparison, some figures and heads he examined carefully through the cup of his hand. Several times he asked at what time of day the picture had been taken, measured shadows, and became more and more deeply immersed.

Once he muttered absently. "One might paint all that."

"Enough!" he finally cried out, and heaved a sigh. "You must tell me much more. It's wonderful having you here! Everything looks different to me now. Come, we'll walk for an hour. I want to show you something."

Aroused, his tiredness gone, he went out, followed by
Burkhardt. First they took the road. Homeward-bound
hay wagons passed in the opposite direction. He
breathed in the warm rich smell of the hay, and a
memory came to him.

"Do you remember," he asked, laughing, "the summer after my first semester at the Academy, when we
were in the country together? I painted hay, nothing
but hay, do you remember? For two weeks I wore
myself out trying to paint some haystacks on a mountain meadow, they just wouldn't come out right, I
couldn't get the color, that dull hay gray! And then
when I finally had it—it still wasn't exactly delicate,
but at least I knew I had to mix red and green—I was
so happy that I couldn't see anything but hay. Oh, what
a wonderful thing it is, that first trying and searching
and finding!"

"It seems to me," said Otto, "that there's always more
to learn."

"Of course. But the things that torment me now have
nothing to do with technique. Do you know, more and
more often in the last few years something I see brings
back my childhood. In those days everything looked
different; one day I hope to put something of that in my
painting. Once in a while I recapture the feeling for a
moment or two, suddenly everything has that special

glow again—but that's not enough. We have so many good painters, sensitive, discriminating men who paint the world as an intelligent, discriminating, unassuming old gentleman sees it. But we have none who paints it as a fresh, high-spirited, imperious boy sees it, and most of those who try to are poor craftsmen."

Lost in thought, he plucked a reddish-blue gypsy rose at the edge of the field and stared at it.

"Am I boring you?" he asked as though suddenly waking, with a diffident look at his friend.

Otto said nothing but smiled.

"You see," the painter went on, "one of the pictures I should still like to paint is a bouquet of wildflowers. My mother, you must know, could make bouquets such as I've never seen since, she was a genius at it. She was like a child, almost always singing, her step was very light and she wore a big brownish straw hat, that's how I always see her in my dreams. Some day I should like to paint a bouquet of wildflowers, the kind she liked: gypsy rose and yarrow, and little pink bindweed, with a few blades of fine grass and a green oat stalk. I've brought home a hundred such bouquets, but they're never quite right, the full fragrance has to be there, it has to be as if she herself had made it. She didn't like white yarrow for instance, she only took the fine rare variety with a dash of violet in it; she would spend half

(47

the afternoon choosing among a thousand blades of grass before selecting one . . . Oh, it's no use, you don't understand."

Burkhardt nodded. "I do understand."

"Yes, sometimes I think of that bouquet for hours on end. I know exactly how the picture ought to be. Not your famous excerpt of nature seen by a good observer and simplified by a skillful energetic painter, and not sweet and sentimental either, as a painter-of-the-native-scene would do it. This picture must be perfectly naïve, as seen through the eyes of a gifted child, unstylized and full of simplicity. The painting in my studio of the fish and the morning fog is the exact opposite—but a painter must be able to do both . . . Oh, I have much more to paint, much more!"

He turned off into a narrow path leading across the meadows, rising gently to a little rounded knoll.

"Now keep your eyes open," he said eagerly, peering ahead like a hunter. "You'll see it from up there! That's what I'm going to paint this fall."

They reached the top. On the far side, a leafy copse traversed by a slanting evening light halted the eye, which, made lazy by the clear open meadow, was slow to find its way through the trees. A path led to a group of tall beech trees with a mossy stone bench under them. Following the path, the eye found an opening; passing the bench, it made its way through a dark passage between treetops into the fresh luminous distance, a valley lined with willow and scrub, the twining river glittering blue-green, and still farther on, chains of hills reaching out to infinity.

Veraguth pointed down. "I'm going to paint that as soon as the beeches take color. I shall sit Pierre down on the bench in the shade so as to look past his head down into the valley."

Burkhardt said nothing. His heart was full of compassion as he listened to his friend. How hard he tries to lie to me, Burkhardt thought with a secret smile. How he speaks of plans and work! He had never done that before. He seemed to be carefully listing the things in which he still took pleasure, that still reconciled him to life. His friend knew him and made no attempt to meet him halfway. He knew that it could not be long before Johann broke a silence that had become unbearable and unburdened himself of everything that had been accumulating over the years. And so he walked along beside him, waiting with apparent serenity, yet inwardly sad, surprised that so superior a man should become such a child in misfortune, as though seeking his way blindfold and with tied hands through brambles.

When on their return to Rosshalde they asked after Pierre, they were told that he had gone to town with Frau Veraguth to meet Herr Albert.

Chapter Four

ANGRILY, ALBERT VERAGUTH PACED THE FLOOR of his mother's music room. At first sight he resembled his father, for he had the same eyes, but in reality he looked far more like his mother, who stood leaning against the piano, following him with affectionate, attentive eyes. When he came close to her, she took him by the shoulders and turned his face to hers. A lock of blond hair hung down over his broad pale forehead, his eyes gleamed with boyish agitation, and his full handsome mouth was twisted with anger.

"No, Mother," he cried, freeing himself from her clasp, "you know I can't go over to see him. That would be sheer comedy. He knows I hate him, and you can say what you like, he hates me too."

"Hate!" she said with gentle severity. "Don't use such words, they distort everything. He is your father and there was a time when he loved you very dearly. I forbid you to speak like that."

Albert stopped still and glared at her.

"Of course you can forbid me to use words, but what does that change? Do you expect me to be grateful to him? He has ruined your life and my home, he has turned our beautiful, happy, wonderful Rosshalde into a place of misery and loathing. I grew up here, Mother, and sometimes I dream night after night of the old rooms and hallways, of the garden and stable and dovecote. I have no other home that I can love and dream of and be homesick for. And now I have to live in strange places and I can't even bring home a friend at vacation time, because I wouldn't want him to see the life we lead! And whenever I meet someone and he hears my name, he sings hymns of praise to my famous father. Oh, Mother, I'd rather we had no father at all and no Rosshalde, I'd rather we were poor people and you had to sew or give lessons, and I'd help you make a living."

His mother took hold of him and pressed him into a chair; she sat down on his knees and stroked his hair into place.

"There," she said in her deep quiet voice, the sound of which was home and hearth to him. "There. Now you've told me everything. Sometimes it's a good idea to get things off your chest. It's good to be conscious of what we have to bear. But we mustn't churn up the things that hurt us, child. You're as tall as I am now, you'll soon be a man, and I'm glad. You are my child and I want you to go on being my child, but you see, I'm alone a good deal of the time and I have all sorts of worries. I need a manly friend, and that must be you.

You must play four-handed with me and stroll in the garden with me and look after Pierre, and we shall have a fine vacation together. But you mustn't fume and fuss and make things still harder for me, because that would make me feel that you were still half a child and that I have a long time to wait for the intelligent friend I want so much."

"Yes, Mother, of course. But when things make me unhappy, must I always keep them to myself?"

"It's the best way, Albert. It's not easy, and one can't expect it of children. But it's the best way. —Shall we play something now?"

"Yes, let's play. Beethoven, the Second Symphony— would you like that?"

They had hardly begun to play when the door opened quietly and Pierre slipped in, sat down on a stool, and listened. He looked thoughtfully at his brother, the back of his neck, the collar of his silk sports shirt, his hair moving to the rhythm of the music, and his hands. Now that the eyes were hidden from him, he noticed Albert's close resemblance to his mother.

"Do you like it?" Albert asked during a pause. Pierre only nodded, but a moment later he quietly left the room. In Albert's question he had sensed a trace of the tone which in his experience most grownups assumed in speaking to children; he could not bear its sham friendliness and ponderous arrogance. He was glad his big brother had come, he had looked forward with eagerness to his visit and had welcomed him joyfully at the station. But that tone, no, he wouldn't put up with it.

Meanwhile, Veraguth and Burkhardt were waiting in the studio for Albert, Burkhardt with unconcealed curiosity, the painter in nervous embarrassment. His brief loquacious gaiety had suddenly left him when he learned that Albert had arrived.

"Is his arrival unexpected?" Otto asked.

"No, I don't believe so. I knew he was coming any day."

Veraguth took some old photographs from a box of odds and ends. He picked out the picture of a little boy and held it side by side with a photograph of Pierre. "This is Albert at exactly the same age that Pierre is now. Do you remember him?"

"Oh, very well. The picture is a good likeness. He looks a good deal like your wife."

"More than Pierre?"

"Yes, much more. Pierre is neither your type nor his mother's. Ah, here he comes. Or is it Albert? No, it can't be."

Light steps were heard outside the door, passing over the flags and the iron foot scraper; the door handle was touched and after brief hesitation turned. In stepped Pierre, darting a friendly, inquiring glance to see if he was welcome.

"Where's Albert?" his father asked.

"With Mama. They're playing the piano."

"I see. He's playing the piano."

"Are you angry, Papa?"

"No, Pierre. I'm glad you've come. What's new?"

The boy saw the photographs and picked them up. "Oh, that's me. And this one? Is it Albert?"

"Yes, that's Albert. That's how he looked when he was exactly your age."

"That was before I was born. And now he's big and Robert calls him Herr Albert."

"Would you like to be grown up?"

"Yes, I would. Grownups can have horses and travel. I'd like to do that. And nobody can call you 'sonny' and pinch your cheeks. But I don't really want to grow up. Old people can be so disagreeable. Even Albert is entirely different now. And when old people get older and older, they die in the end. I'd rather stay the way I am, and sometimes I'd like to be able to fly, and fly around the trees way up high, and in between the clouds. Then I'd laugh at everybody."

"At me too, Pierre?"

"Sometimes, Papa. Old people are so funny sometimes. Mama not so much. Sometimes Mama lies in the garden in a long chair, not doing anything, just looking at the grass; her arms hang down and she's perfectly still and a little sad. It's nice not having to do something all the time."

"Don't you want to be anything? An architect or a gardener, or perhaps a painter?"

"No, I don't want to. There's a gardener here already, and I've got a house. I'd like to do entirely different things. I'd like to understand what the robins say to each other. And I'd like to see how the trees manage to drink water with their roots and get to be so big. I don't think anybody really knows that. The teacher knows a lot, but only boring things."

He had sat down on Otto Burkhardt's lap and was playing with his belt buckle.

"There are many things we can't know," said Burkhardt in a friendly tone. "There are many things we can only see, they're beautiful and we have to be satisfied with that. When you come to see me in India some day, you'll be in a big ship for days and days, lots and lots of little fish jump out of the water ahead of the ship, they have glassy wings and they can fly. And sometimes there are birds that have come a long long way from strange islands; they are very tired, they sit down on the deck and they're very much surprised to see so many strange people riding around on the ocean. They would like to understand us too, and ask us where we come from and what our names are, but they can't, so we just look into each other's eyes and nod our heads, and when the bird has had a good rest, he shakes himself and flies off across the ocean."

"Doesn't anyone know what those birds are called?"

"Oh yes. But we only know the names that people have given them. We don't know what they call each other."

"Uncle Burkhardt has such wonderful stories, Papa. I wish I had a friend too. Albert is too big. Most people don't really understand what I mean when I say something, but Uncle Burkhardt understands right away."

A maid came to take the child away. Soon it was dinner time and the two men repaired to the manor house. Herr Veraguth was silent and out of sorts. In the dining room his son came up to him and they shook hands.

"Good evening, Papa."

"Good evening, Albert. Did you have a good trip?"

"Yes, thank you. Good evening, Herr Burkhardt."

The young man was very cool and correct. He escorted his mother to the table. Dinner was served. The conversation was almost entirely between Burkhardt and the lady of the house. They spoke of music.

"May I ask," said Burkhardt, turning to Albert, "what kind of music you especially like? Though I must admit that I've lost touch, the modern composers are little more than names to me."

The boy looked up politely and replied. "I only know the most modern composers from hearsay myself. I don't belong to any school, I like any kind of music if it's good. Especially Bach, Gluck, and Beethoven."

"Oh, the classics. In our day the only one of those that we knew really well was Beethoven. We had scarcely heard of Gluck. You see, we were all fervent Wagnerians. Johann, do you remember when we heard *Tristan* for the first time? We were carried away!"

Veraguth smiled glumly.

"Old hat!" he cried somewhat harshly. "Wagner is finished. Isn't he, Albert?"

"Oh, not at all. His operas are performed everywhere. But I have no opinion on the subject."

"You don't care for Wagner?"

"I don't know him well enough, Herr Burkhardt. I seldom go to the opera. I'm interested only in pure music, not in opera."

"Well, what about the overture to *Meistersinger!* You must know that. You don't care for that either?"

Albert bit his lips and reflected a moment before answering. "I really have no opinion. It's—how shall I put it—romantic music, it just doesn't interest me."

Veraguth scowled. "Will you have some wine?" he asked by way of a diversion.

(57

"Yes, please."

"And you, Albert? A glass of red wine?"

"Thank you, Papa, I'd rather not."

"Have you become a teetotaler?"

"No, not at all. But wine doesn't agree with me; I'd rather not."

"Very well. But you will drink with me, Otto. Prosit!"

He drained half his glass in one quick gulp.

Albert continued to act the part of a well-behaved young man who has very definite opinions but keeps them modestly to himself, leaving the talking to his elders, not out of eagerness to learn but because he wants to be left alone. The role did not become him, and soon he himself felt quite ill at ease. As usual, he ignored his father as much as possible, wishing to give him no occasion for argument.

Engaged in observing, Burkhardt was silent, so that when the conversation languished in frost, there was no one to revive it. They hurried through the meal, served one another with elaborate politeness, toyed awkwardly with the dessert spoons, and waited in pathetic desolation for the moment when they might leave the table. It was only then that Otto Burkhardt became fully aware of the loneliness and hopeless coldness that had descended on his friend's marriage and life. He glanced toward him, saw him staring in listless gloom at his food, which he scarcely touched, and meeting his eyes for an instant, surprised a look of supplication and of shame at the disclosure of his state.

It was a look of affliction; the loveless silence, the embarrassed coldness and humorless stiffness of this dinner table seemed to proclaim Veraguth's shame aloud. At that moment Otto felt that every additional day he spent at Rosshalde would merely prolong his humiliating role as spectator and the torment of his friend, who by fighting down his loathing was barely able to keep up appearances, but could no longer summon up the strength and spirit to conceal his misery from the onlooker. It was time for him to leave.

No sooner had Frau Veraguth arisen than her husband pushed back his chair. "I'm so tired I must ask you to excuse me. No, no, stay where you are."

He went out, forgetting to close the door, and Otto heard his slow heavy steps receding in the hallway and on the creaking stairs.

Burkhardt closed the door and followed the lady of the house to the drawing room, where the evening breeze was leafing through the music on the still open piano.

"I was going to ask you to play something," he said in embarrassment. "But I believe your husband isn't feeling very well, he was working in the sun half the

E

afternoon. If you don't mind, I think I shall keep him company for a while."

Frau Veraguth nodded gravely and made no attempt to detain him. He took his leave and Albert saw him to the stairs.

Chapter Five

NIGHT WAS FALLING when Otto Burkhardt stepped out of the entrance hall, where the large chandelier had already been lighted, and took his leave of Albert. Under the chestnut trees he stopped, thirstily sucking in the delicately cooled, leaf-scented evening air and wiping great drops of perspiration from his forehead. If he could help his friend a little, this was the time to do it.

There was no light in the painter's quarters; he found Veraguth neither in the studio nor in any of the other rooms. He opened the door on the lake side and with short slow steps made the circuit of the house, looking for him. At length he saw him sitting in the wicker chair he himself had occupied that afternoon while Veraguth was painting him. The painter was huddled forward, his face in his hands, so still that he seemed to be asleep.

"Johann!" Burkhardt called softly, and laid his hand on the bowed head.

Submerged in weariness and suffering, Veraguth did not reply. Burkhardt stood beside him in silence, waiting and stroking his short coarse hair. Only the wind in the trees broke the evening stillness. Minutes passed. Then suddenly through the dusk a great surge of sound came from the manor house, a full, sustained chord and then another—the first measures of a piano sonata.

The painter raised his head, gently shook his friend's hand, and stood up. He looked at Burkhardt silently out of tired, dry eyes, tried to produce a smile, but gave up; his rigid features went slack.

"Let's go in," he said with a gesture, as though to defend himself against the torrent of music.

He went ahead. At the studio door he stopped. "I imagine we won't have you with us much longer?"

How he senses everything! Burkhardt thought. In a controlled voice, he replied: "What's a day more or less? I think I'll be leaving the day after tomorrow."

Veraguth groped for the light buttons. A thin metallic click and the studio was filled with glaring light.

"In that case, let's have a bottle of good wine together."

He rang for Robert and gave him orders. Burkhardt's portrait, almost finished, had been placed in the middle of the studio. They stood looking at it while Robert moved the table and chairs, brought wine and ice, and set out cigars and ashtrays.

"That will do, Robert. You can have the evening off. Don't wake me tomorrow. Leave us now."

They sat down and clinked glasses. The painter squirmed restlessly, stood up, and turned out half the lights. Then he dropped heavily into his chair.

"The picture isn't quite finished," he began. "Take a cigar. It would have been pretty good, but it doesn't really matter. We'll be seeing each other again."

He selected a cigar, cut it with deliberation, turned it between nervous fingers, and put it down again. "You haven't found things in very good shape this time, have you, Otto? I'm sorry."

His voice broke, he huddled forward, reached for Burkhardt's hands, and clasped them firmly in his.

"Now you know it all," he moaned wearily, and a tear or two fell on Otto's hand. But Veraguth was unwilling to let himself go. He straightened up and forced himself to speak calmly. "Forgive me," he said with embarrassment. "Let's have some of the wine. You're not smoking?"

Burkhardt took a cigar.

"Poor fellow!"

They drank and smoked in appeased silence, they saw the light glitter in the crystal glasses and glow more warmly in the golden wine, saw the blue smoke float indecisively through the large room and twist itself into capricious threads. From time to time they ex-

changed a frank, relaxed glance that had little need of
words. It was as though everything had already been
said.

A moth whirred across the studio and struck the
walls three or four times with a dull thud. Then it sat
stupefied, a velvety gray triangle, on the ceiling.

"Will you come to India with me in the fall?" Burkhardt asked at length, hesitantly.

There was another long silence. The moth began to
move about. Small and gray, it crept slowly forward, as
though it had forgotten how to fly.

"Perhaps," said Veraguth. "Perhaps. We must talk
about it."

"Look, Johann. I don't want to torture you. But you
must tell me a certain amount. I never expected that
things would be all right again between you and your
wife, but . . ."

"They were never all right."

"No. But, all the same, I'm aghast at finding them as
bad as this. It can't go on. It's destroying you."

Veraguth laughed harshly. "Nothing is destroying
me, my friend. In September I shall be showing ten or
twelve new paintings in Frankfurt."

"That's fine. But how long can this go on? It's absurd
. . . Tell me, Johann, why haven't you divorced?"

"It's not so simple . . . I'll tell you all about it. You'd
better hear the whole story in the proper order."

He took a sip of wine and continued to lean forward as he spoke, while Otto moved back from the table.

"You know I had difficulties with my wife from the first. For a few years it was bearable, not good, not bad. At that time it might have been possible to save quite a good deal. But I was disappointed and I didn't hide it very well, I kept demanding the very thing that Adele was unable to give. She was never very lively; she was solemn and heavy, I might have noticed it sooner. When there was trouble, she was never able to look the other way or make light of it. Her only response to my demands and my moods, my passionate yearning and in the end my disappointment, was a long-suffering silence, a touching, quiet, heroic patience which often moved me but was no help either to her or to me. When I was irritable and dissatisfied, she suffered in silence, and a little later when I tried to patch things up and come to an understanding, when I begged her to forgive me, or when, in an access of good spirits, I tried to sweep her off her feet, it was no good; she kept silent and shut herself up tighter than ever in her heavy fidelity. When I was with her, she was timid, yielding, and silent, she received my outbursts of rage or of gaiety with the same equanimity, and when I was away from her, she sat by herself, playing the piano, thinking of her life as a young girl. The outcome was that I put myself more and more in the wrong, and in the end I

(65

had nothing more to give or communicate. I became more and more industrious and gradually learned to take refuge in my work."

He was making a visible effort to keep calm. He had no desire to accuse, he wished only to tell his story, but behind his words an accusation was discernible, or at least a plaint at the wrecking of his life, the disappointment of his young hopes, and the joyless half existence, at odds with his innermost nature, to which he had been condemned.

"Even then, I thought of divorce now and then. But it's not so simple. I was used to working in peace and quiet, I couldn't face the thought of courts and lawyers, or of disrupting my daily routine. If a new love had turned up, a decision would have come easily. But my own nature was less resilient than I had thought. I fell in love with pretty, young girls, but what I felt was a kind of melancholy envy; it never went deep enough. I came to realize that there would never again be a love I could abandon myself to as I did to my painting. My need to expend my energies and forget myself, all my passion, went into my painting, and to tell you the truth, I haven't in all these years taken a single new human being into my life, neither a woman nor a friend. You see, any friendship would have had to begin with an admission of my disgrace."

"Disgrace?!" said Burkhardt softly, in a tone of reproach.

"Yes, disgrace! That's how I felt and my feeling hasn't changed. It's a disgrace to be unhappy. It's a disgrace not to be able to show anyone one's life, to be obliged to conceal something. But enough of that! Let me go on."

He stared darkly into his wine glass, tossed away his extinguished cigar, and continued.

"Meanwhile, Albert had grown out of babyhood. We both loved him very much and worrying over him kept us together. It wasn't until he was seven or eight that I began to be jealous and to fight for him—exactly as I fight over Pierre with her now. Suddenly I realized that the little boy had become indispensably dear to me, and then for several years I looked on in constant anguish as he grew cooler and cooler toward me and more and more attached to his mother.

"Then he fell seriously ill, and for a time our worry about the child submerged everything else; we lived in greater harmony than ever before. Pierre dates from that time.

"Since little Pierre has been in the world, he has had all the love it's in me to give. I let Adele slip away from me again; after Albert's recovery, I did nothing to prevent him from growing closer and closer to his mother.

(67

He became her confidant in her conflict with me and soon he was my enemy; in the end I had to send him out of the house. I gave up everything, I became an abject pauper, I stopped finding fault or giving orders in the house, I became a tolerated guest in my own home, but I didn't mind. All I wanted to save for myself was my little Pierre. When life with Albert and the whole state of affairs had become intolerable, I offered Adele a divorce.

"I wanted to keep Pierre with me. She could have everything else: she could live with Albert, she could have Rosshalde and half my income—more, for all I cared. But she refused. She was willing to divorce, she asked only the barest minimum of support, but she would not part with Pierre. That was our last fight. I tried to save my little vestige of happiness; I promised and begged, I humiliated myself, I threatened and wept and in the end I lost my temper; all in vain. She even consented to let Albert go away. It suddenly became clear that this quiet patient woman had no intention of giving an inch; she was well aware of her power and she was stronger than I. At that time I really hated her, and something of that hatred is still with me.

"So I sent for the mason and built this little apartment. I've been living here ever since, and you've seen all there is to see."

Burkhardt had listened thoughtfully, never interrupt-

ing, not even at times when Veraguth seemed to expect
and even to desire it.

"I'm glad," he said cautiously, "that you yourself see
everything so clearly. It's all pretty much as I thought.
Let's talk about it just a little more. You've made a good
start. I've been waiting for this moment ever since I
came, and so have you. Suppose you had a nasty
abscess that was painful and that you were a little
ashamed of. I know about it now, and you feel better
because there's no need for secrecy. But that isn't
enough, now we've got to see if we can't cut the thing
open and heal it."

The painter looked at him, shook his head dully, and
smiled. "Heal it? Such things never heal. But go ahead
and cut."

Burkhardt nodded. Yes, he wanted to cut, he would
not let this hour pass in vain.

"One thing in your story is unclear to me," he said
thoughtfully. "You say it was on Pierre's account that
you didn't divorce your wife. But couldn't you have
forced her to let you have Pierre? If you had gone to
court, they'd probably have had to give you one of the
children. Have you never thought of that?"

"No, Otto, I have never thought of that. It never occurred to me that a judge with his wisdom could repair
my faults and omissions. If I myself hadn't the power
to make my wife give up the boy, there was nothing for

me to do but wait to see in whose favor Pierre would decide later on."

"Then it's all a question of Pierre. If not for him, you would surely have divorced your wife long ago; you'd have found some happiness in the world or at least you'd have worked out a clear and reasonable way of life. Instead, you're caught in a web of compromises, sacrifices, and paltry expedients that can only stifle a man like you."

Veraguth looked up uneasily and gulped down a glass of wine.

"You keep talking about stifling and being destroyed! But you can see that I'm alive and working; I won't let it get me down, I'm damned if I will."

Otto ignored Veraguth's irritation. With gentle insistence he continued. "Excuse me, that's not quite true. You're an uncommonly strong man or you wouldn't have stood up this long under such conditions. You yourself know very well how much this life has hurt you and aged you, trying to hide it from me is useless vanity. When you tell me one thing and my eyes another, I believe my eyes, and I can see that you're in a very bad way. Your work keeps you going, but it's more of an anesthetic than a pleasure. You waste half your magnificent energies in self-denial and petty daily friction. You're not happy, at best you're resigned. And that, my boy, isn't worthy of you."

"Resigned? That may be. A good many people are in that boat. Who's happy?"

"Anyone who has hope is happy!" cried Burkhardt. "And what have you to hope for? Not even outward success, honors, or money; of those you have more than enough. Why, you don't even remember what life and joy are. You're contented, because you've given up hoping. I understand that perfectly, but it's a horrible state to be in, it's a nasty abscess, and anyone who has such a thing and refuses to cut it open is a coward."

He paced the room in violent agitation, and as he pursued his plan with tense energies, Veraguth's boyhood face rose up to him from the depths of memory, recalling a similar quarrel. Raising his eyes, he looked into his friend's face; he was sitting huddled up, peering into space. Every trace of the boyhood features had vanished. He had called him a coward by design. But now this man, formerly so quick to take offense, made no move to defend himself.

He only cried out in embittered weakness: "Go right ahead! No need to spare me. You've seen the cage I live in. Now you can point a finger at my disgrace and rub it in. Please continue. I won't defend myself, I won't even get angry."

Otto stood before him. He felt very sorry for him but forced himself to say harshly: "But you should get angry. You should throw me out and break off our friendship, or else you should admit that I'm right."

Now the painter stood up too, but limply, without vigor. "Very well, you're right, if that's what you want!" he said wearily. "You overestimated me, I'm not as young as I used to be, and not so easy to offend. And I haven't got so many friends that I can afford to throw any away. I have only you. Sit down and have another glass of wine. It's good. You won't get wine like this in India, and perhaps you won't find so many friends out there that will put up with your pigheadedness."

Burkhardt tapped him lightly on the shoulder and said, almost angrily: "Let's not get sentimental, not now of all times. Tell me what fault you have to find with me, and then we'll go on."

"Oh, I have no fault to find with you. You're perfect, Otto, perfect. For almost twenty years now you've watched me going down, you've looked on with friendship and perhaps with regret as I sank deeper and deeper into the swamp, and you've never said anything and never humiliated me by offering me help. For years you knew that I kept a phial of cyanide on me, you observed with noble satisfaction that I didn't take it and finally threw it away. And now that I'm so deep in the muck that I can't get out, you stand there finding fault and giving me advice . . ."

His reddened, feverish eyes stared forlornly. It was

only then that Otto, wishing to pour himself another glass of wine and finding the bottle empty, noticed that Veraguth had drunk up all the wine in those few minutes.

The painter followed his eyes and laughed harshly.

"I'm sorry," he cried angrily. "Yes, I'm a little tipsy, don't forget to take that into account. It happens every few months. I inadvertently get a little drunk . . . I need the stimulation, you see . . ."

Placing his hands heavily on his friend's shoulders, he said plaintively, in a voice grown suddenly high and feeble: "See here, Otto. I might have got along without the cyanide and the wine and all that if someone had offered me a bit of help. Why did you let me sink so far that I have to plead like a beggar for a little indulgence? Adele couldn't bear me, Albert turned away from me, Pierre will leave me too some day—and you stood there, looking on. Couldn't you have done something? Couldn't you have helped me?"

The painter's voice broke, he sank back in his chair. Burkhardt had grown deathly pale. It was much worse than he had thought. That a few glasses of wine could bring this proud, hard man to this unresisting confession of his secret shame and misery!

He stood beside Veraguth and spoke softly to him as to a child in need of comfort. "I'll help you, Johann. Believe me, I'll help you. I've been an ass, I've been blind and stupid. Everything will be all right, don't worry."

He remembered rare occasions in their boyhood when his friend had lost control over his nerves. One such scene, which had lain dormant, deep in his memory, rose up before him in strange clarity. At that time Johann had been going with a pretty girl, a student of painting. Otto had spoken disparagingly of her, and Veraguth had broken off their friendship in the most violent terms. Then too a small amount of wine had affected the painter disproportionately, then too his eyes had turned red and he had lost control over his voice. His friend was strangely moved at this extraordinary recurrence of forgotten traits out of a seemingly cloudless past, and once again he was terrified at the suddenly revealed abyss of inner loneliness and self-torment in Veraguth's life. This no doubt was the secret at which Johann had occasionally hinted over the years, and which, Burkhardt had assumed, lay hidden in the soul of every great artist. This then was the source of the man's uncannily insatiable drive to create, to seize upon the world each hour anew with his senses and to overpower it. And this too was the source of the strange sadness with which great works of art often fill the silent beholder.

It was as though Otto had never fully understood his friend until that moment. Now he saw deep into the dark spring from which Johann's soul drew the strength and suffering in which it was steeped. And at the same time he felt a deep, joyous consolation at the fact that it was he, the old friend, to whom the sufferer had bared himself, whom he had accused, and whom he had begged for help.

Veraguth seemed to have forgotten what he had said. He rested appeased like a child after a tantrum, and finally he said in a clear voice: "You have no luck with me this time. It's all because I haven't been doing my daily work. My nerves are off kilter. Good times don't agree with me."

And when Burkhardt tried to prevent him from opening the second bottle, he said: "I couldn't sleep now anyway. God knows what makes me so nervous. Well, let's just tipple a bit, you weren't so priggish in the old days. —Oh, you mean because of my nerves. I'll straighten them out all right, I've had plenty of experience at that. In the next few days I'll start work every morning at six and every evening I'll ride for an hour."

And so the friends remained together until midnight. Johann talked, turning over memories from the old days, Otto listened, and with almost reluctant pleasure saw a smooth, calm, cheerfully mirroring surface close over the dark depths that had gaped before him only a little while before.

F

Chapter Six

IT WAS NOT WITHOUT UNEASINESS that Burkhardt went to see the painter in the morning. He expected to find his friend changed and feared that his agitation of the night before would have given way to cool irony and embarrassment. Instead, Johann came to meet him with quiet gravity.

"So you're leaving tomorrow," he said. "I understand. And thank you for everything. You know, I haven't forgotten about last night; we shall have to talk some more."

Otto consented, though he had his doubts. "If you like; but I don't want to upset you again for nothing. Maybe we opened up too many wounds last night. Why did we have to wait till the last moment!"

They ate breakfast in the studio.

"No, we did the right thing," said Johann firmly. "Exactly the right thing. I've had a sleepless night and mulled the whole thing over. You opened up a good many wounds, it was almost more than I could bear. Remember, I've had no one to talk to for years. But now I've got to straighten everything out and do what has to be done, or I really am the coward you called me last night."

"Oh, did that hurt? Forget it."

"No, you were almost right, I think. Today I'd like to have one more good happy day with you, we'll go for a drive this afternoon and I'll show you a beautiful piece of country. But first we've got to straighten things out a bit. Yesterday it all came down on me so suddenly that I lost my head. But today I've thought it all over. I think I understand now what you were trying to tell me yesterday."

His manner of speaking was so calm and friendly that Burkhardt's misgivings were dispelled.

"If you understood me, everything is all right and there's no need to start all over from the beginning. You told me how it all came about and how things stand now. Now I see that your only reason for going on with your marriage and household and your whole mode of life is that you don't want to part with Pierre. Am I right?"

"Yes, exactly."

"Well, how do you see the future? I believe you intimated last night that you fear to lose Pierre too in time. Or am I mistaken?"

Veraguth sighed heavily and raised his hand to his forehead; but he continued in the same tone: "That

(77

may be so. That's the sore point. Then you think I ought to give the boy up?"

"Yes, I do. Your wife isn't likely to let you have him and it will cost you years of struggle."

"That may be. But you see, Otto, he's all I've got. I'm living among ruins, and if I died today, no one but you and a few journalists would care. I'm a poor man, but I still have this child, I still have this darling little boy whom I can live for and love, whom I suffer for and with whom in happy hours I can forget myself. You understand that, don't you? And you want me to give him up."

"It's not easy, Johann. It's a bad business. I can't see any other way. Look, you've forgotten what the outside world is like. You sit here buried, engrossed in your work and your unhappy marriage. Take the step, break away from all that; you'll open your eyes and see that the world has thousands of wonderful things to offer you. You've been living with dead things too long, you've lost your contact with life. Of course you're attached to Pierre, he's a delightful child; but that's not the main point. Be a little cruel for once and ask yourself whether he really needs you."

"Whether he needs me . . . ?"

"Yes. What you can give him is love, tenderness, feeling—things that children in general need less of than we old people suppose. And on the other hand the child is growing up with a father and mother who are almost strangers to each other, who are actually jealous of each other on his account. He isn't being educated by the good example of a happy, healthy home, he's precocious, and he'll grow up to be a misfit. —And one day, forgive me, he will have to choose between you and his mother after all. Don't you see that?"

"Perhaps you're right. You're definitely right. But at that point I stop thinking. I'm attached to the child, I cling to his love, because I haven't known any other warmth or light in a long time. Perhaps he will let me down in a few years, perhaps he will disappoint me or even hate me some day—as Albert hates me; once when he was fourteen he threw his jackknife at me. But for a few years I can still be with him and love him, I can take his little hand in mine and listen to his little bright bird-like voice—I still have that. Now tell me: must I give that away? Must I?"

Burkhardt shrugged his shoulders sadly and frowned. "You must, Johann," he said very softly. "I believe you must. It doesn't have to be today, but soon. You must throw away everything you have and wash yourself clean of the past; otherwise you will never again be able to face the world as a free happy man. Do what you can. If the step is too much for you, stay here and go on living this life—I'll still be your friend, you'll still have me, you know that. But I should regret it."

"Give me some advice. I can see nothing but darkness before me."

"I'll give you some advice. This is July; in the fall I shall be going back to India. Before I go, I shall come back here; by then I hope your bags will be packed and you'll be ready to go with me. If by then you've made your decision and say yes, so much the better. But if you haven't made up your mind, come with me and get out of this air for a year, six months if you prefer. With me you'll be able to paint and ride horseback, you'll be able to hunt tigers too and fall in love with Malay women—some of them are pretty—in any case, you'll be away from here for a while, you'll have a chance to see if it isn't a better life. What do you think?"

Eyes closed, the painter rocked his large shaggy head with its pale face and indrawn lips.

"Thank you," he cried with half a smile. "Thank you. You're very kind. In the fall I'll tell you if I'm coming. Please leave the photographs here."

"You can keep them. But—couldn't you make up your mind about the trip today or tomorrow? It would be better for you."

Veraguth rose and went to the door. "No, I can't do that. Heaven knows what will happen between now and then. For years I haven't been without Pierre for more than three, four weeks. I believe I shall go with you but I don't want to say anything now that I might regret."

"Well, we'll let it go at that. You'll always know where to reach me. And if one of these days you wire three words, saying you're coming, you won't have to stir a finger about the trip. I'll attend to everything. Just take some shirts and underwear and painting materials, plenty of those; I'll have everything else sent to Genoa."

Veraguth embraced him in silence.

"You've helped me, Otto. I'll never forget it. —Now I'll send for the carriage, they're not expecting us for meals today. And let's not do anything but enjoy a fine day together, as we used to on our summer vacations. We'll drive through the country, look at a few beautiful villages, and lie in the woods. We'll eat trout and drink good country wine out of thick glasses. How marvelous the weather is today!"

"It hasn't been any different in ten days," Burkhardt laughed. And Veraguth laughed with him.

"Oh, it seems to me the sun hasn't shone like this for years!"

Chapter Seven

AFTER BURKHARDT'S DEPARTURE the painter was overcome by a strange feeling of loneliness. The very same loneliness with which he had lived for years and years, to which by long habituation he had hardened and almost desensitized himself, assailed him like a strange new enemy, moving in on him from all sides to stifle him. At the same time he felt more cut off from his family than ever, and even from Pierre. He did not know it, but the reason was that he had spoken of these things for the first time.

At times he even became acquainted with the wretched, humiliating feeling of boredom. Until then Veraguth had lived the unnatural but consistent life of a man who, having immured himself of his own free will, had lost interest in life, which he endured rather than lived. His friend's visit had pierced his wall; through a hundred chinks the sound and glitter, the fragrance and feel of life penetrated to the lonely man; an old spell was broken, and as he waked, the call from outside rang loudly and half painfully in his ears.

He flung himself furiously into his work, starting two large compositions at almost the same time. He began his day with a cold bath at sunrise and worked without pause until noon; after a short rest he revived himself with coffee and a cigar, and sometimes awoke at night with palpitations and a headache. But drive and discipline himself as he would, he carried with him, obscured by only the lightest of veils, the awareness that a door was open and that one quick step could carry him to freedom whenever he chose.

He did not think about it, he deadened his thoughts with constant work. His feeling was: you can go at any time, the door is open, your shackles can be broken—but it will cost you a hard decision and a heavy, heavy sacrifice—so don't think about it, above all don't think about it! The decision which Burkhardt expected of him, and which inwardly he had perhaps already made, was lodged in his mind like a bullet in the flesh of a wounded man; the question was only whether it would work its way out of the suppurating sore or become more and more firmly embedded. It festered and ached, but it did not yet hurt him enough; the pain he feared from his sacrifice was still too great. So he did nothing; he let his hidden wound burn, and all the while he was desperately curious to know how it would all end.

In the midst of his affliction he painted a large composition; the plan had long been present in his mind, but now suddenly it fascinated him. At first, some years ago, he had taken pleasure in the idea, then it had come to seem more and more empty and allegorical, and at length to repel him altogether. But now he saw the whole picture clearly; the allegory was forgotten, and he set to work with the vision fresh before him.

There were three life-sized figures: a man and a woman, each self-immersed and alien to the other, and between them, playing, a child, tranquilly happy and without suspicion of the cloud hanging over him. The personal significance was clear, but the man neither resembled the painter nor the woman his wife; the child, however, was Pierre, though a few years younger. He painted this child with all the charm and nobility of his best portraits; the figures at either side sat in rigid symmetry, severe sorrowful images of loneliness, the man heavily brooding, his head resting in one hand, the woman lost in suffering and dull emptiness.

Life was none too pleasant for Robert, the servant. Herr Veraguth had grown strangely irritable. He could not bear the slightest sound in the next room when he was working.

The secret hope that had come alive in Veraguth since Burkhardt's visit was like a flame in his breast; repress it as he might, it went on burning, coloring his dreams at night with an alluring, exciting light. He tried to ignore it, to banish it from his thoughts, he wanted only to work with peace in his heart. But he found no peace. He felt the ice of his joyless existence melting and all the foundations of his life tottering; in his dreams he saw his studio closed and empty, he saw his wife traveling away from him, but she had taken Pierre with her, and the boy held out his thin arms to him. Sometimes in the evening he sat for hours alone in his uncomfortable living room, immersed in the Indian photographs; then at length he would thrust them aside and close his tired eyes.

Within him two powers carried on a hard struggle, but hope was the stronger. Over and over again he had to repeat his conversations with Otto; with ever increasing warmth the repressed desires and needs of his vigorous nature rose up from the depths where they had so long lain frozen and imprisoned, and this upsurge, this spring thaw got the better of his old illusion, the sick illusion that he was an old man who could do no more than endure life. The deep, potent hypnosis of resignation had been broken, and through the breach poured the unconscious instinctual forces of a life long curbed and cheated.

The more clearly he heard the voices, the more he trembled inwardly in dread fear of the final awakening. Time and again he closed his dazzled eyes as every feverish fiber of his being rebelled against the necessary sacrifice.

Johann Veraguth seldom showed himself in the manor house, he had nearly all his meals brought to the studio and often spent his evenings in town. But when he did meet with his wife or Albert, he was quiet and gentle and appeared to have forgotten all his hostility.

He seemed to take little interest in Pierre. Formerly he had lured the child to the studio at least once a day and kept him there or gone out into the garden with him. Now whole days would pass without his seeing the child or craving his presence. When the boy crossed his path, he kissed him thoughtfully on the forehead, looked into his eyes with absent sadness, and went his way.

One afternoon Veraguth went to the chestnut grove. A balmy wind was blowing, and a warm rain slanted down in tiny drops. Music resounded from the open windows of the house. The painter stopped still and listened. He did not know the piece. It sounded pure and grave in its strict, well-constructed, well-balanced beauty, and Veraguth listened with thoughtful pleasure. Strange, this seemed to be music for old people; it sounded so adult and forbearing, with none of the Bacchic frenzy of the music he had loved beyond everything else in his youth.

Quietly he stepped into the house, mounted the stairs, and appeared soundless and unannounced in the music room, where only Frau Adele noticed his coming.

Albert was playing and his mother stood listening at the piano; Veraguth sat down in the nearest chair, bowed his head, and went on listening. From time to time he looked up and let his eyes rest on his wife. This was her home, in these rooms she had spent quiet disillusioned years as had he in his studio by the lake, but she had had Albert, she had grown with him, and now their son was her guest and friend, he was at home with her. Frau Adele had aged slightly, she had learned to live quietly and had found contentment; her expression had grown rigid and her mouth somewhat set; but she was not uprooted, she lived secure in her own atmosphere, and it was in her atmosphere that her sons were growing up. She had little exuberance or impulsive tenderness, she was lacking in almost everything that her husband had sought in her and hoped for, but around her it was home, there was character in her face, in her presence, in her rooms; this was a soil in which children could grow up and gratefully thrive.

Veraguth nodded as though with satisfaction. Here there was no one who could lose by it if he disappeared forever. In this house he was not indispensable. He would be able to build a studio anywhere in the world and surround himself with activity and his passion for work, but it would never be a home. Actually he had known that all along, and it was just as well.

Albert stopped playing. He felt, or he saw in his

mother's eyes, that someone had entered the room. He turned around and looked at his father with surprise and mistrust.

"Good afternoon," said Veraguth.

"Good afternoon," his son replied, with embarrassment, and began to busy himself at the music cabinet.

"You've been playing?" Veraguth asked amiably.

Albert shrugged his shoulders as though to ask: Haven't you heard? He blushed and hid his face deep in the shelves of the cabinet.

"It was beautiful," Veraguth continued, smiling. He was keenly aware that his visit was unwelcome; he said with a certain malicious pleasure: "Won't you play something else? Whatever you like. You've made good progress."

"Oh, I'm not in the mood any more," said Albert irritably.

"I'm sure it will go very well. Please do."

Frau Veraguth looked at her husband inquiringly.

"Come along, Albert, sit down," she said, setting a book of music on the rack. As she did so, her sleeve grazed a little silver vase filled with roses, and a few pale petals fell on the black, highly polished wood.

The boy seated himself on the piano stool and began to play. Bewildered and angry, he reeled off the music like a tedious exercise, fast and unlovingly. For a time his father listened attentively, then he sank into thought, and at length he stood up and left the room without a sound before Albert had finished. Once outside, he heard the boy hammer furiously on the keys and stop playing.

"They won't miss me at all when I'm gone," the painter thought as he descended the stairs. "Good Lord, how far apart we are, and yet we were once a family of sorts."

In the hallway Pierre ran toward him, beaming and very much excited.

"Oh, Papa," he cried breathlessly, "I'm glad you're here. Guess what, I've got a mouse, a little live mouse! Look, here in my hand—can you see his eyes? The yellow cat caught him, she was playing with him, she tortured him, she kept letting him run a little way and then she caught him again. So I reached out quick, quick, and snatched the mouse out from under her nose. What shall we do with him now?"

He looked up, glowing with pleasure, but shuddered as the mouse struggled in his small, tightly closed hand, emitting short frightened squeaks.

"We'll take him out to the garden and let him go," said his father. "Come along."

He provided himself with an umbrella and took the boy out with him. The sky had grown brighter and the rain had subsided to a drizzle; the wet smooth trunks of the beech trees glistened black like cast iron.

They stopped in a spot where the roots of several trees formed a hard intricate tangle. Pierre crouched down and very slowly opened his hand. His face was flushed and his light gray eyes flashed with excitement. Then suddenly, as though his expectation had become too great for him to bear, he opened his hand wide. The mouse, a tiny little creature, shot blindly out of his prison, stopped a few feet away beside a great knot of roots, and sat there quietly, his flanks heaving and his shining little black eyes darting fearfully this way and that.

Pierre cried out for joy and clapped his hands. The mouse took fright and vanished as though by magic into the ground. Gently, the father stroked the child's thick hair.

"Will you come with me, Pierre?"

The child put his right hand in his father's left and went with him.

"Now the little mouse is home with his papa and mama, telling them all about it."

The words bubbled out of him and the painter held his warm little hand tightly. With every word and joyful cry the child uttered, his heart quivered and sank back into servitude to the heavy charm of love.

Oh, never again in his life would he experience such love as he did for this child. Never again would he know moments so full of glowing warm tenderness, so full of playful self-forgetfulness, of poignant, melancholy sweetness as with Pierre, this last lovely image of his own youth. His charm, his laughter, his self-possessed freshness were, so it seemed to Veraguth, the last note of pure joy in his life, the last flowering rosebush in an autumnal garden. In it lingered warmth and sunshine, summer and pastoral joy, but when storm or frost stripped its petals, then all delight, every intimation of happiness would be at an end.

"Why don't you like Albert?" Pierre asked suddenly.

Veraguth pressed the child's hand more tightly. "I do like him. It's just that he loves his mother more than he does me. I can't help that."

"I think he doesn't like you at all, Papa. And do you know, he doesn't like me as much as he used to, either. He's always playing the piano or sitting alone in his room. The first day he came, I told him about my garden that I had planted myself, and all he did was make a high-and-mighty face and say: 'Very well, we'll go and look at your garden tomorrow.' But he hasn't mentioned it the whole time. He's not a good friend, and besides he's beginning to have a little mustache. And he's always with Mother, I can hardly ever have her to myself."

"But he'll only be here for a few weeks, my boy, don't forget that. And if you don't find Mama alone, you can always come and see me. Don't you like to?"

G

"It's not the same, Papa. Sometimes I like to go and see you and sometimes I'd rather see Mama. And besides, you always have to work so terribly hard."

"You mustn't let that worry you, Pierre. When you feel like seeing me, you can always come—always, do you hear, even if I'm in the studio working."

The boy made no answer. He looked at his father, sighed a little, and looked dissatisfied.

"Doesn't that suit you?" Veraguth asked, distressed by the expression on the child's face, which only a moment ago had shone with boyish high spirits but now looked withdrawn and much too old.

He repeated his question. "Speak up, Pierre. Aren't you pleased with me?"

"Of course I am, Papa. But I don't really like to go and see you when you're painting. I used to now and then . . ."

"Well, and what displeased you?"

"You know, Papa, when I go and see you in the studio, you always stroke my hair and you don't say anything and you have entirely different eyes, and sometimes they're angry. Yes. And then if I say something, I can see by your eyes that you're not listening, you just say yes, yes, and you don't pay attention. And when I come and want to tell you something, I want you to listen to me."

"All the same, you must come again, sweetheart. You

see, if I'm thinking hard about my work and I have to rack my brains about the best way of doing something, then sometimes I can't shake myself free right away and listen to you. But I'll try the next time you come."

"Yes, I understand. It's the same with me. Sometimes I'm thinking about something and somebody calls me and I'm supposed to come—it's beastly. Sometimes I want to be still and think all day, and that's just when I have to play or study or do something, and then I get very angry."

Pierre looked off into space, straining under his effort to express his meaning. It was hard, and most of the time no one understood you anyway.

They had entered Veraguth's living room. He sat down and held the child between his knees. "I know what you mean, Pierre," he said soothingly. "Would you like to look at pictures now, or would you rather draw? Why couldn't you draw the story of the mouse?"

"Oh yes, I'll do that. But I'll need a nice big sheet of paper."

Veraguth took a sheet of drawing paper from the table drawer, sharpened a pencil, and pulled up a chair for the boy.

Kneeling on the chair, Pierre began at once to draw the mouse and the cat. Not to disturb the child, Veraguth sat behind him, watching his thin, sunburned neck, his graceful back, and aristocratic, willful

(93

head. Pierre was deep in his work, which he accompanied with impatient lip movements. Every line, every successful or unsuccessful stroke, was clearly reflected in his restless lips, in the movements of his eyebrows and the creases in his forehead.

"Oh, it's no good," Pierre cried out after a time. Straightening up and propping his cheeks on his open hands, he examined his drawing with a critical frown.

"It's not getting anywhere," he said with plaintive impatience. "Papa, how do you make a cat? Mine looks like a dog."

His father took the paper and inspected it earnestly.

"We'll have to erase a little," he said gently. "The head is too big and not round enough, and the legs are too long. Wait, we'll get it."

Cautiously, he ran his eraser over Pierre's paper, took a fresh sheet, and drew a cat on it.

"Look. This is how it must be. Look at it for a moment, and then draw a new cat."

But Pierre's patience was exhausted, he gave back the pencil, and now his father had to draw, after the cat, a little kitten, then a mouse, then Pierre coming and setting the mouse free, and then finally the child demanded a carriage with horses and a coachman on the box.

Then suddenly that bored him too. Singing, the boy

ran about the room, looked out the window to see if it was still raining, and danced out the door. His frail high voice could be heard singing under the windows, and then there was silence. Veraguth sat alone, holding the sheet of paper with the cats on it.

Chapter Eight

V ERAGUTH STOOD FACING HIS LARGE CANVAS with the three figures, working on the woman's light bluish-green dress. On her throat a small gold ornament glittered sad and forlorn, alone to catch the precious light which found no resting place on the shaded face and glided alien and joyless over the cool blue dress . . . the selfsame light which played gaily and tenderly in the blond tousled hair of the beautiful child beside her.

There was a knock at the door. The painter stepped back in irritation. When after a brief wait the knocking was repeated, he strode to the door and opened it a crack.

There stood Albert, who had not set foot in the studio since the start of his vacation. Holding his straw hat in hand, he looked rather uncertainly into his father's tense face.

Veraguth let him in.

"Hello, Albert. I suppose you've come to look at my pictures. There isn't much here."

"Oh, I didn't wish to disturb you. I only wanted to ask you . . ."

But Veraguth had closed the door and had gone past the easel to a gray-painted rack where his pictures were standing in tall narrow drawers equipped with rollers. He pulled out the painting with the fishes.

Albert stood awkwardly beside his father and both looked at the silvery-shimmering canvas.

"Are you interested in painting?" Veraguth asked airily. "Or do you care only for music?"

"Oh, I'm very fond of painting, and this one is beautiful."

"You like it? I'm glad. I'll have a photograph of it made for you. And how does it feel to be back in Rosshalde?"

"Thank you, Papa, it feels wonderful. But I really didn't want to disturb you. I only came to ask you . . ."

The painter was not listening. With the groping, rather strained expression that he always had when working, he looked absently into his son's face.

"Tell me, how do you young people feel about art these days? I mean, do you hold with Nietzsche, or do you still read Taine—he was intelligent, I've got to admit, but boring—or have you new ideas?"

"I haven't read Taine yet. I'm sure you've thought about such things a lot more than I have."

"Formerly, yes, art and culture, and the Apollonian and the Dionysian and all that, seemed terribly important. But today I'm satisfied if I can turn out a good

0

picture, I don't see problems any more, in any case not philosophical problems. If I had to tell you why I'm a painter and why I spread paint on canvas, I should say: I paint because I have no tail to wag."

Albert looked with astonishment at his father, who had not spoken to him like this in a long time. "No tail? What do you mean?"

"It's very simple. Dogs and cats and other talented animals have tails; their tails, with their thousands of flourishes, provide them with a wonderfully complete language of arabesques, not only for what they think and feel and suffer but for every mood and vibration of their being, for every infinitesimal variation in their feeling tone. We have no tails, and since the more lively among us need some such form of expression, we make ourselves paintbrushes and pianos and violins . . ."

He broke off as though suddenly losing interest in the conversation, or as though it had just dawned on him that he was talking alone, meeting with no real response in Albert.

"Well, thank you for your visit," he said abruptly.

He had gone back to his canvas and taken up his palette, and was staring searchingly at the spot where he had made his last brush stroke.

"Excuse me, Papa, I wanted to ask you something . . ."

Veraguth turned around; already his eyes were remote, he had lost contact with everything outside his work.

"Yes?"

"I'd like to take Pierre for a drive in the carriage. Mama said I could but she wanted me to ask you."

"Where do you want to go?"

"A few hours' drive in the country, maybe to Pegolzheim."

"I see . . . Who's going to drive?"

"Me, of course, Papa."

"All right, you may go with Pierre. But take the coupé and the bay. And see that he doesn't get too much oats."

"Oh, I'd much rather take the carriage and pair."

"I'm sorry. When you're alone, you can do as you please, but when the little fellow's with you, you've got to take the bay."

Somewhat disappointed, Albert withdrew. At other times he would have argued or pleaded, but he saw that the painter was once more absorbed in his work, and here in the studio, amid the aura of his paintings, his father, for all the boy's inner resistance, still made a powerful impression on him. Elsewhere he did not recognize his father's authority, but here he felt pitifully boyish and weak in his presence.

Instantly, the painter was deep in his work, the interruption was forgotten, the outside world had vanished. With intense concentration he compared the canvas with the living picture within him. He felt the music of the light, how its resounding stream dispersed and came together again, how it flagged on meeting resistance, how it was absorbed but triumphed invincibly anew on every receptive surface, how it played on the colors with capricious but infallibly precise sensibility, intact despite a thousand refractions and in all its playful meanders unswervingly faithful to its inborn law. And with relish he breathed the heady air of art, the bitter joy of the creator who must give himself till he stands on the brink of annihilation, and can find the sacred happiness of freedom only in an iron discipline that checks all caprice and gains moments of fulfillment only through ascetic obedience to his sense of truth.

It was strange and sad, but no more strange and sad than all human destiny: this disciplined artist, who derived his power to work from the deepest truthfulness and from clear uncompromising concentration, this same man in whose studio there was no place for whim or uncertainty, had been a dilettante in his life, a failure in his search for happiness, and he, who never sent a bungled drawing or painting out into the world, suffered deeply under the dark weight of innumerable bungled days and years, bungled attempts at love and life.

Of this he was not conscious. For years he had not felt the need to see his life clearly. He had suffered and resisted suffering in rebellion and resignation, but then he had taken to letting things ride and saving himself for his work. With grim tenacity, he had almost succeeded in giving his art the richness, depth, and warmth that his life had lost. And now, girded in loneliness, he was as one enchanted, enmeshed in his artistic purpose and uncompromising industry, too healthy and resolute to see or recognize the poverty of such an existence.

This is how it had been until recently, when his friend's visit had shaken him up. Since then the lonely man had lived with a foreboding of danger and impending fate, of struggles and trials in which all his art and industry could not save him. In his damaged humanity he sensed that a storm was in the offing and that he lacked the roots and inner strength to withstand it. And in his loneliness he accustomed himself only very slowly to the thought that he would soon have to drain the cup of suffering to the lees.

Fighting off these dark forebodings, living in dread of decisions or even of clear ideas, the painter summoned up all his energies as though for a last great exertion, very much as a pursued animal musters every ounce of strength for the leap that will save it. And so, in those days of inner anguish, Johann Veraguth, by a desperate effort, created one of his greatest and most beautiful works, the playing child between the bowed and sorrowful figures of his parents. Standing on the same ground, bathed in the same air and light, the figures of the man and woman breathed death and bitterest coldness, while between them, golden and jubilant, the child gleamed as though in a blissful light of his own. And when later, Veraguth's modest judgment to the contrary, some of his admirers numbered him among the truly great, it was largely because of this picture into which he had breathed all the anguish of his soul, though intending nothing more than a piece of perfect craftsmanship.

In those hours Veraguth knew nothing of weakness and fear, of suffering, guilt, and failure in life. Neither joyful nor sad, wholly absorbed by his work, he breathed the cold air of creative loneliness, desiring nothing of a world he had forgotten. Quickly and surely, his eyes protruding with concentration, he laid on color with little sharp thrusts, gave a shadow greater depth, made a swaying leaf or a playful lock of hair hover more softly and freely in the light. He gave no thought to what his picture expressed. That lay behind him; it had been an idea, an inspiration; now he was concerned not with meanings, feelings, or thoughts, but with pure reality. He had gone so far as to attenuate and almost obliterate the expression of the faces, he had no desire to tell a story; the fold of a cloak gathered around a knee was as important and sacred to him as a bowed forehead or a closed mouth. The picture was to make nothing visible but three human figures seen purely as objects, connected with one another by space and air, yet each surrounded by the unique aura that disengages every deeply seen image from the world of irrelevant relationships and calls forth a tremor of astonishment at its fateful necessity. Thus from the paintings of dead masters, over-life-size strangers whose names we do not know and do not wish to know look out at us enigmatically as symbols of all being.

The picture was far advanced, almost completed. He had left the finishing touches on the charming figure of the child for the last; he would work on it tomorrow or the day after.

It was well past lunchtime when the painter felt hungry and looked at his watch. He washed in haste, dressed, and went to the manor house, where he found his wife alone at table and waiting.

"Where are the boys?" he asked in surprise.

"They've gone for a drive. Didn't Albert drop in to see you?"

It was only then that he remembered Albert's visit. Distracted and somewhat embarrassed, he began to eat. Frau Adele watched him wearily and absently cutting his meat. She had rather given up expecting him. The strain in his features touched her with a kind of compassion. She served him in silence and poured wine for him, and he, sensing a vague friendliness, made an effort to say something pleasant.

"Does Albert mean to become a musician?" he asked. "I believe he has a good deal of talent."

"Yes, he is gifted. But I don't know if he's cut out for an artist. I don't believe he wants to become one. So far, he hasn't shown much enthusiasm for any profession, his ideal is to be a kind of gentleman who would engage in sports and studies, social life and art all at once. I don't see how he can make a living that way, I shall have to make that clear to him little by little. Meanwhile he works hard and has good manners, I shouldn't like to upset him and worry him needlessly. After graduating from school he wants to do his military service first, in any case. After that, we shall see."

The painter said nothing. He peeled a banana and took pleasure in the mealy, nutritious smell of the ripe fruit.

"If it doesn't inconvenience you, I should like to take my coffee here," he said finally. His tone was friendly, considerate, and a trifle weary, as though it would soothe him to rest here and enjoy a little comfort.

"I'll have it brought in. —Have you been working hard?"

That had slipped out almost unawares. She meant

nothing by it; she wished only, since it was a moment of unusual pleasantness, to show a little interest, and that did not come easy, she had lost the habit.

"Yes, I've been painting for a few hours," her husband answered dryly.

It disturbed him that she should ask. It had become customary between them that he did not speak of his work, there were many of his more recent paintings that she had never seen.

She felt that the bright moment was slipping away and did nothing to hold it. And he, who was already reaching for his cigarette case and about to ask leave to smoke, lost his desire and let his hand drop.

But he drank his coffee without haste, asked a question about Pierre, thanked his wife politely, and stayed on another few minutes, contemplating a small painting he had given her some years before.

"It holds up rather well," he said, half to himself. "It still looks pretty good. Except for the yellow flowers, they shouldn't really be there, they draw too much light."

Frau Veraguth made no reply; it so happened that the delicate, finely painted yellow flowers were what she liked best in the picture.

He turned around with a shadow of a smile. "Goodbye; don't let the time hang too heavy on your hands until the boys get back."

Then he left the room and descended the stairs. Outside, the dog jumped up on him. He took his paws in his left hand, stroked him with his right hand, and looked into his eager eyes. Then he called through the kitchen window for a piece of sugar, gave it to the dog, cast a glance at the sunny lawn, and went slowly back to the studio. It was a fine day to be out of doors, the air was marvelous; but he had no time, his work was waiting for him.

There stood his painting in the quiet diffused light of the high studio. On a green surface dotted with a few wildflowers sat the three figures: the man bent over, deep in hopeless brooding, the woman waiting in resigned and joyless disillusionment, the child bright and guileless, playing in the flowers; and over them all an intense, vibrant, triumphantly flowing light glittered with the same carefree warmth in every flower as in the boy's luminous hair and in the little gold ornament on the disconsolate woman's throat.

Chapter Nine

THE PAINTER HAD WORKED ON TOWARD EVENING.
Now, deadened with fatigue, he sat for a while in
his armchair, his hands in his lap, utterly drained, with
slack cheeks and slightly inflamed eyelids, old and
almost inert, like a peasant or woodcutter after heavy
toil.

He would have liked best to remain in his chair and
surrender to his fatigue and craving for sleep. But habit
and stern discipline would not let him; after ten or
fifteen minutes he jolted himself awake. He stood up
and without so much as a glance at the painting went
down to the landing, undressed, and swam slowly
around the lake.

It was a milky-pale evening; muffled by the woods,
the sound of creaking hay wagons and the weary cries
and laughter of farm hands returning from the day's
work could be heard from the nearby road. Veraguth
stepped shivering out of the water, carefully rubbed
himself warm and dry, went into his little living room,
and lighted a cigar.

He had planned to write letters this evening, now he

H

opened his desk drawer without conviction, but irritably closed it again and rang for Robert.

The servant appeared.

"Tell me, when did the boys get back with the carriage?"

"They didn't, Herr Veraguth."

"What, they're not back yet?"

"No, Herr Veraguth. I only hope Herr Albert hasn't tired the bay too much. He tends to be a little hard on the horses."

His master did not answer. He would have liked to spend half an hour with Pierre, who, he supposed, had returned long ago. Now he was angry and rather frightened at the news.

He ran across to the manor house and knocked at his wife's door. There was astonishment in her answer, he never came to see her at this hour.

"Excuse me," he said, repressing his agitation, "but where is Pierre?"

Frau Adele looked at her husband with surprise. "The boys have gone for a drive, don't you remember?" Sensing his irritation, she added: "You're not worried?"

He shrugged his shoulders impatiently. "No. But it's thoughtless of Albert. A few hours, he said. He might have phoned at least."

"But it's still early. They'll surely be back before dinner."

"The little fellow is always gone when I want to spend a little time with him."

"There's no point in getting excited. These things happen. Pierre spends plenty of time with you."

He bit his lips and left without a word. She was right, there was no point in getting excited, there was no point in being intense and demanding anything of the moment. It was better to sit there patient and indifferent as she did.

Angrily, he went downstairs and out through the gate to the road. No, that was something he had no desire to learn, he wanted his joy and his anger. What a damper this woman had already put on him, how temperate and old he had become, he who had formerly prolonged happy days boisterously into the night and smashed chairs in anger. All his bitterness and resentment rose up in him, and at the same time an intense longing for his boy, whose voice and glance alone could give him joy.

With long strides, he started down the road. A sound of wheels was heard, and eagerly he hastened his step. It was nothing. A peasant with a cart full of vegetables. Veraguth called out to him. "Have you passed a coupé with two boys on the box?"

The peasant shook his head without stopping, and his lumbering farm horse jogged on indifferently into the mild evening.

As he walked, the painter felt his anger cool and seep away. His step became more relaxed, a soothing weariness came over him, and as he strode easily along, his eyes rested gratefully on the rich quiet countryside, which lay pale and mild in the misty evening light.

He was hardly thinking of his sons when, after he had been walking for half an hour, their carriage came toward him. It was close to him before it caught his attention. Veraguth stopped under a large pear tree. When he recognized Albert's face, he stepped back, not wishing them to see him and call out to him.

Albert was alone on the box. Pierre sat slumped in a corner of the carriage, his bare head had drooped and he seemed to be asleep. The carriage rolled past and the painter looked after it, standing at the side of the dusty road until it disappeared from sight. Then he turned around and started back. He would have liked to see Pierre, but it was almost the child's bedtime and Veraguth had no desire to show himself at his wife's house that day.

And so, passing the park, the house, and the gate, he continued on into town, where he took supper at a tavern and leafed through the papers.

By then his sons had long been home. Albert sat with

his mother, telling her about the expedition. Pierre had been very tired, he had not wanted his supper, and now he was lying asleep in his pretty little bedroom. When his father passed the house on his way home, there was no light to be seen. The balmy starless night surrounded park, house, and lake with black stillness, and fine soft raindrops fell from the motionless air.

Veraguth put on the light in his living room and sat down at his desk. His craving for sleep was gone. He took a sheet of letter paper and wrote to Otto Burkhardt. Little moths flitted in through the open windows. He wrote:

My dear friend:
You were probably not expecting a letter from me so soon. But since I am writing now, you surely expect more than I can give. You think that clarity has come to me and that I now see the damaged mechanism of my life as neatly in cross section as you believe you see it. Unfortunately, that is not the case. Yes, there have been flashes of summer lightning inside me since we spoke of those things, and from time to time an extremely painful revelation stares me in the face; but it is not daylight yet.

So, you see, I can't say what I shall or shall not do later on. But we will go away together. I will go to India with you, please get me a berth as soon as you know the date. I can't leave before the end of the summer, but in the fall the sooner the better.

I want to give you the painting you saw here, the one with the fishes, but it would please me to have it stay in Europe. Where shall I send it?

Here everything is as usual. Albert is playing the sophisticated gentleman, you can't imagine how respectfully we treat each other, like the ambassadors of two hostile powers.

Before we leave, I shall expect you again at Rosshalde. I must show you a painting that will be finished any day now. It's good work, a good thing to wind up my career with in case your crocodiles gobble me up, which, I have to admit, would displease me in spite of everything.

I must go to bed now, though I am not sleepy. I was at my easel for nine hours today.

Your Johann

He addressed the letter and put it out in the hall for Robert to take to the post office next day.

Looking out of the window before getting into bed, the painter heard the whishing of the rain that he had disregarded while writing. It descended in soft swathes from the darkness and for a long time he lay awake listening as it fell in little tinkling streams from the sodden foliage to the thirsty earth.

Chapter Ten

PIERRE IS SO TEDIOUS, said Albert to his mother as they went out into the rain-fresh garden to cut roses. "He hasn't paid much attention to me the whole time, but yesterday I couldn't get *anything* out of him. A few days ago when I suggested going for a drive together, he was full of enthusiasm. But yesterday he didn't really want to go, I almost had to plead with him. It wasn't much fun for me, not being able to take the two horses, I really went mostly for his sake."

"Wasn't he well behaved?" Frau Veraguth asked.

"Oh, very well behaved, but so tedious. There's something so blasé about him sometimes. No matter what I suggested or showed him or offered him, I could hardly get a smile or an 'Oh, yes' out of him. He didn't want to sit on the box, he didn't want to learn how to handle the reins, he didn't even want to eat apricots. He was like a spoiled little prince. It was annoying; I'm telling you because I really don't want to take him out with me any more."

His mother stopped still and looked at him searchingly; his eyes flashed with indignation and she could not repress an amused smile.

"My big baby," she said soothingly. "You must have patience with him. Perhaps he wasn't feeling very well, he hardly ate a thing for breakfast this morning. That happens now and then with all children, it was the same with you. It usually comes from an upset stomach or from bad dreams at night, and it's true that Pierre is rather frail and sensitive. And besides, he may be a little jealous. Don't forget that he usually has me all to himself, and now you're here and he has to share me with you."

"But it's my vacation! He must realize that, he's not stupid!"

"He's a little boy, Albert. You'll just have to be more intelligent than he is."

Rain was still dripping from the fresh, metallically glistening leaves. They had come to pick the yellow roses that Albert was especially fond of. He bent the crowns of the bushes apart and his mother with her garden shears cut the flowers, which still drooped a little, weighed down by the rain.

"Was I like Pierre when I was his age?" Albert asked thoughtfully.

Frau Adele tried to remember. Lowering the hand that held the shears, she looked into her son's eyes and then closed her own, trying to evoke his image as a child.

"You looked a good deal like him except for the eyes,

but you weren't so tall and thin, you started growing a little later."

"And the rest? My character, I mean."

"Well, my boy, you too had your moods. But I think you were steadier, you didn't jump from one game or occupation to another as quickly as Pierre does. And he's more emotional than you were, not as well balanced."

Albert took the shears from his mother's hand and bent over a rose bush. "There's more of Papa in Pierre," he said softly. "Isn't it strange, Mother, how the qualities of parents and grandparents, or a mixture of them, recur in children? My friends say that every child has all the elements in him that will shape his whole life, and that there's nothing to be done about it, absolutely nothing. For instance, if somebody has the makings of a thief or murderer, it just can't be helped, he'll be a criminal and that's that. It's horrible. You believe it, don't you? It's absolutely scientific."

"That may be," Frau Adele smiled. "When a person becomes a thief or a murderer, scientists may be able to prove that he has always had it in him. But I'm sure there are lots of good straight people who have inherited plenty of evil from their parents and grandparents and go on being good all the same, but science can't very well investigate that. I should say that good will and a good upbringing are more reliable than heredity. We all know what's good and right, or we can learn, and that's what we've got to go by. Nobody knows exactly what hereditary mysteries any man has inside him, and it's best not to worry too much about them."

Albert knew that his mother never let herself in for dialectical arguments, and instinctively he felt that her naïve reaction was right. Yet he knew that this was not the last word on the frightening subject, and he would have liked to say something decisive about the theory of causality, which had seemed so convincing when some of his friends had spoken of it. He cast about in vain for clear, compelling formulations, though—unlike those friends, whom he nevertheless admired—he felt that at heart he inclined far more to an ethical or aesthetic attitude than to the objective, scientific view which he professed among his fellow students. In the end, he let the matter drop and turned back to the roses.

Meanwhile, Pierre, who was indeed not feeling well and had awakened much later than usual and without zest, had stayed in his room with his toys until he began to feel bored. He was quite wretched, and it seemed to him that something special must happen to make this lackluster day bearable and just a little pleasant.

Hesitating between anticipation and distrust, he left the house and went to the lime grove in search of something new, some discovery or adventure. He had a dismal feeling in his stomach; that had happened before, but never had his head felt so tired and heavy. He would have liked to run to his mother and cry. But that was impossible in the presence of his big proud brother, who always, even on normal days, made it plain that he was still a little boy.

If only it occurred to his mother to do something, to call him and suggest a game and be nice to him. But of course she had gone off with Albert again. Pierre felt that this was an unlucky day, that there was little to hope for.

Listless and dejected, he sauntered along the gravel paths, his hands in his pockets, chewing on the withered stem of a lime blossom. It was damp and morning cool in the garden and the stem had a bitter taste. He spat it out and stopped still, thoroughly out of sorts. He couldn't think of anything, today he felt like being neither prince nor bandit, neither ferryman nor builder.

Frowning, he looked about on the ground, poked at the gravel with the tips of his shoes, kicked a gray slimy slug off the walk and into the wet grass. Nothing would speak to him, no bird or butterfly, nothing would smile at him and beguile him into gaiety. Everything was silent, everything looked drab and hopeless. He tried a little shiny-red currant from the first bush he passed; it tasted cold and sour. It would be good to lie down and sleep, he thought, and not wake up until everything looked new and beautiful and happy again. There was no point in wandering around like this, making himself miserable and waiting for things that were not going to happen. How lovely it would be, for instance, if a war had broken out and a lot of soldiers came up the road on horseback, or if a house was on fire somewhere or there was a big flood. Ah, such things only happened in picture books, in real life you never got to see them, maybe they didn't even exist.

Sighing and woebegone, the child sauntered on; the light had gone out of his fine, handsome face. When he heard the voices of Albert and his mother behind the trellis, he was so overcome with jealousy and rancor that the tears rose to his eyes. He turned around and went away very quietly for fear they would hear him and call out to him. He didn't want to answer, he didn't want anybody to make him speak and pay attention and be good. He was feeling so wretched and nobody cared; well, then he wanted at least to savor his loneliness and sadness and feel really miserable.

He remembered God-in-His-heaven, whom at times he thought very highly of; the thought brought a remote glimmer of comfort and warmth, but it soon vanished. Probably God-in-His-heaven was a fake too. And yet, now more than ever, he would have been so glad to have someone he could rely on, someone with something pleasant and comforting to offer.

Then he thought of his father. Perhaps, he felt hopefully, perhaps his father would understand him, because he himself usually looked still and tense and unhappy. His father would surely be standing in his big quiet studio, painting his pictures, he always was. It wasn't really a good idea to disturb him. But he had said only very recently that Pierre should always come to see him when he felt like it. Perhaps he had forgotten, grownups always forgot their promises so quickly. But there was no harm in trying. Heavens, no, since he could think of no other consolation and needed one so badly.

Slowly at first—then, as his hopes rose, more briskly —he went down the shaded walk to the studio. He put his hand on the latch and stood still, listening. Yes, his father was inside, he could hear him breathing and clearing his throat, and he heard the delicate wooden click of the brush handles he was holding in his left hand.

Cautiously he pressed the latch, opened the door without a sound, and looked in. He recoiled at the strong smell of turpentine and varnish, but his father's broad powerful frame aroused hope. Pierre went in, closing the door behind him.

At the click of the latch, the painter's broad shoulders, closely observed by Pierre, quivered, and he turned his head. There was an injured, questioning look in his sharp eyes, and his mouth hung open unpleasantly.

Pierre stood motionless. He looked into his father's eyes and waited. Instantly the eyes became friendlier and the irritation went out of the painter's face. "Well, if it isn't Pierre! We haven't seen each other in a whole day. Did Mama send you?"

The child shook his head and let his father kiss him.

"Would you like to stay here a while and watch?" his father asked in a friendly tone. He turned back to his painting and aimed a little pointed brush at a certain spot. Pierre watched. He saw the painter study his canvas, saw his eyes staring intensely and almost angrily and his strong nervous hand aiming the brush, saw him frown and bite his lower lip. And he smelled the pungent studio air, which he had always hated and which was especially repugnant to him that day.

The light went out of his eyes and he stood by the door as though paralyzed. He knew all this, the smell and his father's eyes and those grimaces of concentration, and he knew it had been silly to expect this day to be different from any other day. His father was working, he was deep in his foul-smelling paint, all he could think of was his stupid paintings. It had been silly to come.

The boy's face fell in disappointment. He had known

it all along! There was no refuge, not with his mother, and certainly not here.

For a long moment he stood vacuous and sad, looking at the large painting with its glistening wet paint, but seeing nothing. His papa had time for that, but not for him. He put his hand on the latch and pressed it down, meaning to slip away quietly.

But Veraguth heard the timid sound. He looked around, grumbled, and went over to the child. "What's the matter, Pierre? Don't run away. Don't you want to stay here with your papa awhile?"

Pierre withdrew his hand and nodded feebly.

"Is there something you wanted to tell me?" the painter asked affectionately. "Come, we'll sit down together. Then you'll tell me. How was your drive yesterday?"

"Oh, it was nice," said Pierre like a well-behaved child.

Veraguth ran his hand through the child's hair. "Didn't it do you good? You're looking kind of sleepy, my boy. They didn't by any chance give you wine to drink yesterday? No? Well, what shall we do now? Shall we draw?"

"I don't feel like it, Papa. It's so dull today."

"Really? You didn't sleep well, that must be it. How about some gymnastics?"

Pierre shook his head. "I don't feel like it. I just want to be with you. But it smells so bad here."

Veraguth caressed him and laughed. "That really is bad luck, not liking the smell of paint when you're a painter's child. I suppose you don't ever want to be a painter?"

"No, I don't."

"What do you want to be?"

"Nothing. I'd like best to be a bird or something like that."

"That wouldn't be bad. But tell me, sweetheart, what you want of me. You see, I've got to work on this big picture. If you like, you can stay here and play. Or shall I give you a picture book to look at?"

No, that was not what he wanted. Just to get away, he said he would go and feed the pigeons, and it did not escape him that his father was relieved to see him go. He was dismissed with a kiss and went out. His father closed the door and Pierre was alone again, feeling emptier than ever. He ambled across the lawn, where he was not really supposed to go, and absently and dolefully broke off a flower or two. He saw that the wet grass had spotted and darkened his light tan shoes, but he didn't care. Finally, overcome with despair, he flung himself down in the middle of the lawn, sobbing and burying his head in the grass. He could feel the water-soaked sleeves of his light-blue blouse sticking to his arms.

It was only when he began to shiver that he calmed down and crept timidly back into the house.

Soon they would call him; they would see he had been crying, they would see his wet, dirty blouse and his damp shoes, and scold him. They were all enemies. He slipped past the kitchen door, he didn't want to meet anyone now. He wished he were somewhere far away where no one knew him and no one would ask after him.

Then he saw the key in the door of one of the rarely occupied guest rooms. He went in and shut the door; then he closed the open windows and without taking his shoes off clambered, wild with fatigue, up on the large bed, which had not been made up. There he lay in his misery, half weeping, half dozing. When after a long time he heard his mother calling him from the yard, he did not answer but buried himself obstinately in the blanket. His mother's voice came and went and finally died away; he could not bring himself to answer. At last he fell asleep, his cheeks bathed in tears.

The moment Veraguth came in to lunch, his wife asked: "Haven't you brought Pierre with you?"

The note of anxiety in her voice did not escape him.

"Pierre? I don't know where he is. Hasn't he been with you two?"

I

Frau Adele was frightened; her voice rose. "No, I haven't seen him since breakfast. When I looked for him, the girls said they had seen him on his way to the studio. Hasn't he been there?"

"Yes, he was there, but only for a moment, then he ran away." And, angrily, he said: "Doesn't anybody in this house look after the boy?"

Frau Adele was offended. "We thought he was with you," she said curtly. "I'll go and look for him."

"Send someone else. Lunch is on the table."

"You can start. I shall look for him."

She hurried out of the room. Albert stood up and was going to follow her.

"Albert, you stay here," cried Veraguth. "We are at table."

The young man looked at him angrily. "I'll eat with Mother," he said in a tone of defiance.

Veraguth looked at his flushed face and smiled ironically. "Very well. You're the master here, aren't you? And, by the way, if you feel like throwing any more knives at me, don't let any old-fashioned prejudices deter you."

Albert blanched and pushed back his chair. This was the first time his father had brought up his act of childish rage.

"You have no right to speak to me like that," he shouted. "I won't stand for it!"

Veraguth did not answer. He picked up a piece of bread and bit into it. He filled his glass with water and drank it slowly, determined to keep calm. He pretended he was alone. Albert went irresolutely to the window.

"I won't stand for it!" he shouted again, unable to repress his anger.

His father sprinkled salt on his bread. In his thoughts he saw himself boarding a ship and riding over endless strange oceans, far away from this incurable confusion.

"Never mind," he said, almost peacefully. "I see you don't like me to talk to you. All right, let's drop it."

At that moment a cry of astonishment and a flood of excited words were heard. Frau Adele had discovered the boy in his hiding place. The painter hurried out. Everything seemed to be going wrong today.

He found Pierre lying with his soiled shoes on the rumpled guest-room bed. His face was sleepy and tear-stained, his hair in disorder. Beside him stood Frau Adele, helpless in her consternation.

"But, child," she cried at length, torn between worry and anger, "what are you doing? Why don't you answer? And why are you lying here?"

Veraguth lifted the child up and looked anxiously into his expressionless eyes. "Are you sick, Pierre?" he asked tenderly.

The boy shook his head in bewilderment.

"Have you been sleeping here? Have you been here long?"

With a thin, frightened voice, Pierre said: "I can't help it . . . I didn't do anything . . . I just had a headache."

Veraguth carried him to the dining room.

"Give him a dish of soup," he said to his wife. "You must eat something hot, child, it will make you feel better, you'll see. Poor little fellow, you must be sick."

He sat him down, wedged a cushion behind his back, took a spoon, and fed him soup.

Albert sat silent and reserved.

"He really seems to be sick," said Frau Veraguth, almost relieved, after the manner of a mother who is more cheerfully prepared to care for illness than to investigate and deal with unaccustomed misconduct.

"We'll put you to bed in a little while, just eat now, my darling," she comforted him.

Pierre's face was gray. He sat there with half-closed eyes and swallowed without resistance what was spooned into him. While his father fed him his soup, his mother felt his pulse and was reassured to find that he had no fever.

"Should I get the doctor?" asked Albert in an unsteady voice, feeling that he ought to be doing something.

"No, never mind," said his mother. "Pierre is going to

bed, we'll bundle him up nice and warm. He'll have a good night's sleep and tomorrow he'll be all right. Won't you, angel?"

The child was not listening. He shook his head when his father tried to give him more soup.

"No, he mustn't force himself," said his mother. "Come along, Pierre, we'll go to bed and everything will be all right."

She took him by the hand. He stood up sleepily and followed his mother. But in the doorway he stopped, grimaced, doubled up, and in a fit of nausea vomited everything he had eaten.

Veraguth carried him to his room and left him to his mother. Bells rang, servants ran upstairs and down. The painter ate a few bites. In between he ran once or twice to see Pierre, who had been undressed and washed and now lay in his brass bed. Then Frau Adele came back and reported that the child was quiet, that he felt no pain and apparently wanted to sleep.

Veraguth turned to Albert: "What did Pierre have to eat yesterday?"

Albert recollected, but addressed his answer to his mother. "Nothing special. In Brückenschwand I gave him bread and milk, then for lunch in Pegolzheim we had chops and macaroni."

The father went on with his inquisition. "And later?"

"He didn't want anything more to eat. In the afternoon I bought him some apricots from a gardener. He only ate one or two."

"Were they ripe?"

"Yes, of course. You seem to think I'm to blame for his upset stomach."

The mother saw the boy's irritation and asked: "What's wrong with you two?"

"Nothing," said Albert.

Veraguth continued: "I don't think anything. I'm only asking. Didn't anything happen yesterday? Didn't he vomit? Or did he fall down? Didn't he complain of pains?"

Albert replied with a curt yes or no, wishing desperately for this meal to be over.

Returning again to Pierre's room, on tiptoe, Veraguth found him asleep. His pale little face had the gravity of utter abandonment to consoling sleep.

Chapter Eleven

O N THAT ANXIOUS DAY Johann Veraguth completed his large painting. Frightened and deeply
troubled on leaving the sick child, he had found it
harder than ever to hold his thoughts in check and to
capture the perfect peace of mind which was the secret
of his strength and for which he had to pay so high a
price. But his will was strong, he succeeded, and that
afternoon, in the fine soft light, he put the finishing
touches to his work.

When he laid aside his palette and sat down facing
the canvas, he felt strangely desolate. He knew that this
picture was good, that he had produced something
remarkable. But inwardly he was empty, burned out.
And he had no one to whom he could show his work.

His friend was far away, Pierre was sick, and there
was no one else. The only reactions that would reach
him—in newspapers and letters—were those of an
indifferent outside world. They meant nothing, less
than nothing; at that moment, only the glance of a
friend or the kiss of a loved one could have rewarded
him, given him pleasure and strength.

For some minutes he gazed in silence at the picture,

which, having absorbed the energies and the good hours of his past few weeks, radiated vitality, while he stood there exhausted and estranged.

"Oh, well, I'll sell it, it will pay for my trip to India," he said in defenseless cynicism. He closed the doors of his studio and went over to the manor house to see how Pierre was getting along. He found him asleep. The boy looked better than at lunch time, sleep had brought color to his face, his mouth was half open, the expression of torment and hopelessness had vanished.

"How quickly these things pass with children," he whispered to his wife in the doorway. She smiled feebly and he saw that she too had been relieved of a weight, that her worry had been greater than she had shown.

The thought of dinner alone with his wife and Albert did not appeal to him.

"I shall be going to town," he said. "I won't be here this evening."

Pierre lay dozing, his mother darkened the room and left him.

He dreamed that he was walking slowly through the flower garden. Everything looked different, much bigger and wider than usual; he walked and walked and there was no end. The flower beds were more beautiful than he had ever seen them, but the flowers all seemed strangely glassy, large, and unfamiliar, and the whole gleamed with a sad dead beauty.

Somewhat uneasy, he walked around a circular bed of shrubs with large blossoms. A blue butterfly clung, quietly sucking, to a white flower. It was unnaturally still, on the walks there was no gravel but something soft, it was like walking on a carpet.

From the other side of the flower bed, his mother came toward him, but she did not see him and did not nod to him; she looked severely and sadly into the air and passed soundlessly by, like a ghost.

A little while later, on another path, he saw his father, and then Albert, and they too walked straight ahead, silent and severe, and neither of them saw him. Under enchantment, they went about stiff and solitary, and it seemed as though it must always be like this, as though there would never be a light in their fixed eyes or a smile on their faces, as though no sound would ever be wafted into this impenetrable silence or the softest breeze ever touch the motionless leaves and branches.

The worst of it was that he himself was unable to call out. There was nothing to prevent him, he felt no pain, but he had no courage and no real desire to; he understood that this was how it had to be, and that it would only be more horrible if he rebelled.

Pierre went slowly on through the soul-less splendor of the garden. Thousands of magnificent flowers glittered in the bright dead air, as though they were not real or alive. From time to time he saw Albert or his mother or father, and always they passed him and one another with the same unrecognizing rigidity.

It seemed to him that this had been going on for a long time, years perhaps, and that those other times, when the world and the garden had been alive, when people had been cheerful and talkative and he himself full of joy and wildness, lay far far away in a deep blind past. Perhaps the world had always been as it was now, and the earlier life was only a pleasant, foolish dream.

At length he came to a little stone basin where the gardener had formerly filled his watering cans and where he himself had kept a few tiny tadpoles. The bright green water stood motionless, reflecting the stone rim and the overhanging leaves of a clump of yellow asters. It looked pretty, forsaken, and somehow unhappy like everything else.

"If you fall in there, you drown and you're dead," the gardener had once said. But it wasn't at all deep.

Pierre stepped up to the edge of the oval basin and bent forward.

He saw his own face mirrored in the water. It was like the faces of the others: old and pale and rigid with severity and indifference.

He was surprised and horrified, and suddenly the secret dread and meaningless sadness of his condition rose up in him overpoweringly. He tried to cry out, but there was no sound. He wanted to wail, but all he could do was screw up his face and grin helplessly.

Then his father reappeared and Pierre turned to him, desperately summoning up all his strength. He sobbed silently, and all his anguish, all the unbearable suffering of his despairing heart, turned to his father for help. His father approached as impassive as a ghost and again seemed not to see him.

"Father!" the child tried to cry out, and although no sound could be heard, the force of his terrible affliction reached the silent, solitary man. His father turned his face and looked at him.

With a painter's searching look, he peered attentively into the imploring eyes, smiled feebly, and gave a slight nod; there was kindness and regret in his glance but no solace, as though there were nothing to be done. For a brief moment a shadow of love and of kindred suffering passed over his severe face, and in. this brief moment he was no longer the all-powerful father, but rather a poor helpless brother.

Then again he looked straight ahead and went slowly on at the same even pace.

Pierre saw him recede and disappear, the basin and the path and the garden grew dark before his horrified eyes and vanished like misty clouds. He awakened with aching temples and a hot parched throat and saw that he was lying in bed alone in the darkened room. He tried in amazement to think back, but found no memories. Exhausted and discouraged, he turned over on the other side.

Full consciousness returned to him only slowly. Then he sighed with relief. It was ugly to be sick and have a headache, but it was bearable; it was light and sweet compared to the deathly feeling of his nightmare.

What was the good of all this torment, Pierre thought, and rolled himself up into a ball under his blanket. What was the point in sickness? If it was a punishment—what was he being punished for? He hadn't even eaten anything forbidden—as he had once, when he had spoiled his stomach eating unripe plums. They were forbidden, but he had eaten them all the same; so it had served him right and he had had to take the consequences. That was plain. But now? Why was he lying in bed now, why had he had to vomit, and why did he have such a wretched pain in his head?

He had been lying awake for a long time when his mother came into the room. She opened the curtain and the room was flooded with soft evening light.

"How are you, darling? Have you had a good sleep?"

He did not answer. Lying on his side, he raised his eyes and looked up at her. She looked back at him in surprise. His eyes seemed strangely questioning and grave.

No fever, she thought with relief.

"Would you like something to eat now?"

Pierre shook his head feebly.

"Isn't there something I can bring you?"

"Water," he said softly.

She brought him water, but he took only a sip, then he closed his eyes again.

Suddenly the piano rang out from next door, filling the room with great waves of sound.

"No!" he cried out. "No! Leave me alone!"

He held both hands over his ears and burrowed his head in the pillow.

With a sigh, Frau Veraguth went to her room and asked Albert to stop playing. Then she came back and sat at Pierre's bedside until he dozed off again.

That evening it was very still in the house. Veraguth was absent, Albert was disgruntled at not being able to play the piano. They went to bed early. Frau Veraguth left her door open so as to hear Pierre if he needed anything during the night.

Chapter Twelve

O N HIS RETURN FROM TOWN that night, Veraguth had made his way stealthily past the house, on the alert for a lighted window, an opening door, or a voice that would tell him his darling was still sick and suffering. Finding all quiet and asleep, he felt his fear fall from him like a heavy wet garment, and was deeply thankful as he lay in bed awake. Shortly before he finally fell asleep, he smiled to think how little it took to cheer a dejected heart. Everything that tormented him and weighed him down, the whole dismal sodden burden of his life turned to nothing, became light and insignificant beside his loving anguish over his child, and no sooner had that dark shadow receded than everything looked brighter and his whole life seemed bearable.

Next morning he awoke in good spirits and went to the manor house at an unusually early hour. Gratified to find Pierre still blissfully asleep, he breakfasted alone with his wife—Albert was not up yet. For years Veraguth had not appeared at Frau Adele's table at this hour, and she eyed him with almost distrustful surprise as he asked her matter-of-factly but with friendly good humor for a cup of coffee and shared her breakfast as in the old days.

At length he noticed her uneasiness and realized how unusual it was for him to appear at this time of day.

"I'm so glad," he said, in a voice that reminded his wife of better years. "I'm so glad the little fellow seems to be on the mend. It has only just come to me that I was seriously worried about him."

"Yes," she agreed, "I wasn't at all pleased with him yesterday."

He played with his silver coffee spoon and gave her an almost mischievous look, a faint reflection of the boyish gaiety—suddenly erupting and soon passing— which was one of the qualities that had most endeared him to her in times gone by; a fragile glow which only Pierre had inherited.

"Yes," he began cheerfully, "it's really a blessing. And now I can finally discuss my latest plans with you. I think you ought to take both boys to St. Moritz this winter for a long stay."

She looked down uncertainly.

"And you?" she asked. "Do you mean to paint up there?"

"No, I won't go with you. I'm going to leave you all to yourselves for a while, and take a trip. I'm planning to leave here in the fall and close up the studio. I'll give Robert a vacation. It's entirely up to you, you can spend the winter here at Rosshalde if you like. I wouldn't advise it. Better go to Geneva or Paris, and don't forget St. Moritz, it will be good for Pierre."

She looked up at him, perplexed. "You're joking," she said incredulously.

"Oh no," he said with a half-melancholy smile. "I've lost the habit. I'm serious and you've got to believe me. I'm going on an ocean voyage. I shall be away for some time."

"An ocean voyage?"

She tried hard to collect her thoughts. His suggestions, his hints, his cheerful tone—all this was unaccustomed and made her distrustful. But suddenly the words "ocean voyage" aroused an image: she saw him boarding a ship, followed by porters with suitcases; she remembered the posters of steamship companies and the Mediterranean cruises she herself had taken, and in a moment she understood it all.

"You're going with Burkhardt!" she cried.

He nodded. "Yes, I'm going with Otto."

Both were silent for a time. She sensed the significance of the announcement and was dismayed. Did he intend to leave her, to set her free? In any case, it was his first serious move in that direction and she was terrified to note how little emotion, how little alarm or hope she felt at the prospect, and no joy whatever. For him perhaps a new life was possible, for her it was not.

She would have an easier time of it with Albert; she would win Pierre, yes; but she would always be a forsaken woman. She had thought of this possibility a hundred times, she had seen it as a promise of freedom and salvation; but now that it seemed as though the possibility might become reality, there was so much anxiety and shame and sense of guilt bound up with it that she lost hope and was capable of no desire. It should have happened sooner, she felt, in the days of storm and acute unhappiness, before she had learned resignation. Now it came too late, it was useless, it was no more than a line under finished business, a conclusion and bitter confirmation of everything she had concealed and only half admitted to herself; it no longer held a spark of new life.

Veraguth read his wife's controlled features attentively and he felt sorry for her.

"We'll give it a try," he said appeasingly. "You'll live together undisturbed, you and Albert—and Pierre, too—for about a year, let's say. I thought it would be convenient for you, and it would certainly be a good thing for the children. It weighs on them a bit that . . . that we haven't managed our life so very well. And we ourselves ought to see things more clearly after a prolonged separation. Don't you think so?"

"Perhaps," she said softly. "Your mind seems to be made up."

K

"I've written Otto. It's not easy for me, you know, to leave you all for so long."

"Pierre, you mean."

"Yes, especially Pierre. I know you'll take good care of him. I can't expect you to speak to him very much about me. But don't let it be the same with him as with Albert."

She shook her head in protest. "I wasn't to blame for that. You know I wasn't."

Cautiously, he rested his hand on her shoulder, with awkward, long-unpracticed tenderness.

"Oh, Adele, let's not talk about blame. Let's say that I'm to blame for everything. I only want to make amends, nothing more. I'm only asking you not to let me lose Pierre if it can be helped. He is still a tie between us. Just see to it that his love for me isn't made too hard for him."

She closed her eyes as though to guard herself against a temptation.

"But if you stay away so long . . ." she said hesitantly. "He's a child . . ."

"Of course. Let him go on being a child. Let him forget me if there's no other way. But remember, he's a pledge that I'm leaving with you and, remember, I must trust you very much to be able to leave him with you."

"I hear Albert coming," she whispered quickly. "He will be here in a moment. We shall talk some more later on. It's not as simple as you think. You give me freedom, more than I've ever had or wanted, and at the same time you give me a responsibility that deprives me of all sense of freedom. Let me think about it some more. You yourself didn't make this decision in an hour; give me a little time too."

Steps were heard outside the door and Albert came in.

Surprised to see his father sitting there, he greeted him with constraint, gave Frau Adele a kiss, and sat down to breakfast.

"I have a surprise for you," said Veraguth amiably. "You can spend your autumn vacation with Mama and Pierre wherever you like, and Christmas vacation too. I shall be away for several months."

The boy could not conceal his joy, but he made an effort and said with enthusiasm: "Where are you going?"

"I don't know yet exactly. First I'm going to India with Burkhardt."

"Oh, so far away? A school friend of mine was born there, in Singapore, I think. They still hunt tigers there."

"I hope so. If I shoot one, I'll bring back the skin of course. But mostly I want to paint."

"I should think so. I've read about a French painter who was somewhere in the tropics, on some island in the South Seas, I think . . . it must be wonderful."

"That's just what I think. And in the meantime you will be happy and play a lot of music and ski. But now I'm going to see what the little fellow's doing. Don't get up."

He was gone before anyone had answered.

"Sometimes Papa is marvelous," said Albert in his joy. "A trip to India! I like that. That has style."

His mother smiled with difficulty. Her balance had been shaken, she felt as though she were sitting on a limb that was being sawed off. But she smiled and composed a friendly expression; she was practiced at that.

The painter had gone into Pierre's room and sat down at his bedside. He quietly took out a little sketchbook and began to draw the little sleeper's head and arm. He had no wish to torment the child with sittings, but was resolved to sketch him as often and as well as possible in the days remaining, and so imprint him on his memory. With tender care he studied the beloved forms, the slope and parting of the delicate hair, the graceful nervous nostrils, the slender, inertly resting hand, and the willful, aristocratic line of the firmly closed mouth.

He seldom saw the child in bed, and never before had he seen him sleeping other than with childlike open lips. Observing the precocious, expressive mouth, he was struck by its resemblance to that of his own father,

Pierre's grandfather, who had been a spirited and imaginative but passionately restless man. As he watched the child and sketched, he mulled over this meaningful game that nature plays with the features and destinies of fathers, sons, and grandsons, and the troubling, fascinating riddle of necessity and chance grazed the mind of this man who was not a thinker.

Suddenly the sleeper woke up and looked into his father's eyes, and again Veraguth was struck by the grave, unchildlike quality of that glance and that awakening. He had quickly put away his pencil and closed his sketchbook. Now he bent over the child, kissed him on the forehead, and said gaily: "Good morning, Pierre. Are you feeling better?"

The child smiled happily and began to stretch. Oh yes, he felt better, much better. Little by little, he remembered. Yes, yesterday he had been sick, he could still feel the menacing shadow of the ugly day. But now things were much better, he just wanted to lie in bed a little longer, to savor its warmth in quiet thankfulness, then he would get up and have breakfast and go out into the garden with Mama.

Veraguth went to get Mama. Pierre looked blinking toward the window; the bright joyful daylight was shining through the pale yellow curtains. Now here was a day that held out some promise, that was fragrant with every pleasure. How shallow and cold and heavy it had been yesterday! He closed his eyes in order to forget it, and felt smiling life stretching in his sleep-sluggish limbs.

And now his mother came in with an egg and a cup of milk, and his father promised him new colored crayons, and they were all loving and affectionate, happy to see him well again. It was almost like a birthday, and it didn't matter that there was no cake, because he wasn't really hungry yet.

As soon as he was dressed, in a fresh blue summer suit, he went to see Papa in the studio. He had forgotten yesterday's ugly dream, but there was still a faint, trembling echo of dread and suffering in his heart, and now he had to see and savor the sunshine and love around him, and make sure they were really there.

His father, who was measuring the frame for his new painting, was overjoyed to see him. But Pierre wasn't meaning to stay very long, he only wanted to say good morning and let himself be loved a little. Then he had to go on, to see the dog and the pigeons and Robert and take a look at the kitchen, and greet them all again and take possession of them again. Then he went out into the garden with Mama and Albert, and it seemed to him that a year had passed since he had lain there in the grass weeping. He didn't feel like swinging, but he put his hand on the swing. Then he went to see the shrubs and flower beds, and a dark memory as of a former life came to him, as though he had once been lost here among the flower beds, lost, forsaken, and disconsolate. Now everything was bright and alive again, the bees were buzzing and the air was light and joyful to breathe.

His mother gave him her flower basket to carry, she put in carnations and big dahlias, and meanwhile he made a separate bouquet, he would take it to his father later.

When they returned to the house, he was tired. Albert offered to play with him, but he wanted to rest a little first. Still holding Papa's bouquet, he sank deep into his mother's big wicker chair on the veranda. Feeling agreeably weary, he closed his eyes, turned toward the sun, and took pleasure in the red warm light shining through his lids. Then he looked happily down over his pretty, clean suit and held his glistening yellow shoes out into the sunlight, alternating right and left. He found it pleasant to sit so quietly and a little languidly in comfort and cleanliness; only the scent of the carnations was too strong. He set them down and pushed them across the table, as far as his arm would reach. He would have to put them in water soon, or else they would fade before Papa saw them.

He thought of his father with unusual tenderness. Now what had happened yesterday? He had gone to see him in the studio, Papa had been working and hadn't

(145

had time, he had been standing at his picture, alone and hard at work and a little sad. So far, he could remember everything exactly. But then what? Hadn't he met his father in the garden later on? He tried to remember. Yes, his father had been walking back and forth in the garden, alone and with a strange, unhappy face, he had wanted to call out to him . . . What had happened? Something horrid or frightening had happened yesterday, or he had heard about it yesterday, and he couldn't find it again.

Leaning back in the deep chair, he followed his thoughts. The sun shone yellow and warm on his knees, but very gradually his happiness left him. He felt that his thoughts were coming closer and closer to that horrid thing, and he felt that as soon as he found it, it would have power over him again; it was standing behind him, waiting. Whenever his memory approached that dividing line, a feeling of nausea and dizziness rose up in him, and his head began to ache.

The carnations bothered him with their overpowering smell. They were lying on the sunny wicker table and fading; if he wanted to give them to his father, now was the time. But he no longer felt like it, or, rather, he felt like it but he was so tired and the light hurt his eyes. And most of all, he had to think and remember what had happened yesterday. He felt that he was very close to it, that his thoughts had only to reach out for it, but each time it vanished and was gone.

His headache got worse. Oh, why did it have to be? He had been so happy today.

Frau Adele called his name from the doorway and a moment later she came out. She saw the flowers lying in the sun and was going to send Pierre for water, but then she looked at him and saw him slumped down in the chair with great tears on his cheeks.

"Pierre, child, what's the matter? Aren't you feeling well?"

He looked at her without moving and closed his eyes again.

"Answer me, angel, what's the matter? Do you want to go to bed? Shall we play a game? Are you in pain?"

He shook his head and made an unfriendly face, as though she were molesting him.

"Leave me alone," he whispered.

And when she straightened him up and threw her arms around him, he flared up for a moment as if in anger and screamed in an unnaturally high voice: "Oh, leave me alone!"

An instant later his resistance ceased, he sank down in her arms, and when she picked him up, he moaned feebly, let his pale face droop forward, and writhed in a fit of vomiting.

Chapter Thirteen

SINCE VERAGUTH HAD BEEN LIVING ALONE in the new wing of his studio, his wife had never been to see him there. When she rushed into the studio without knocking, he was immediately prepared for bad news. So sure was the warning of his instinct that before she could say a word, he blurted out: "Is there something wrong with Pierre?"

She nodded hurriedly. "He must be seriously ill. He was acting very strangely, and now he has vomited again. You must go for the doctor."

As she spoke, her eyes darted through the large room and came to rest on the new painting. She did not see the figures, she did not even recognize little Pierre, she only stared at the canvas and breathed in the air of this place where her husband had been living all these years. Dimly she sensed an atmosphere of loneliness and defiant self-sufficiency not unlike that in which she herself had been living so long. The impression of a moment, then she turned away from the painting and tried to answer her husband's headlong questions.

"Phone for the motorcar," he said at length. "That will be quicker than the carriage. I'll go to town myself, just let me wash my hands. I'll be right over. You've put him to bed?"

Fifteen minutes later he was in town, looking for the only doctor he knew, who had made one or two calls at the house some years before. Veraguth went to the doctor's old address but found that he had moved. On his way to the new address, he passed the doctor's carriage, the doctor greeted him, he replied, and had already passed before it came to him that this was the man he was looking for. He turned around and found the doctor's carriage drawn up outside a patient's house. After an exasperatingly long wait, he caught the doctor in the doorway and made him get into the motorcar. The doctor objected and resisted, Veraguth almost had to use force.

In the motorcar, which started for Rosshalde at top speed, the doctor laid his hand on his knee and said: "Very well, I'm your prisoner. Others who need me will have to wait, you know that. Now tell me what the trouble is. Is your wife ill? —No? —The little boy then? What's his name again? Ah yes, Pierre. I haven't seen him in a long time. What's wrong? Has he had an accident?"

"He's sick, it started yesterday. This morning he seemed to be all right again, he was up and ate a little. But just now he started vomiting again and he seems to be in pain."

HERMANN HESSE

The doctor passed his thin hand over his ugly-intelligent face. "Must be his stomach. We'll see. Is everything else all right? I saw your show in Munich last winter. We're proud of you, my friend."

He looked at his watch. They were both silent as the gears were shifted for the grade and the chugging of the engine grew louder. They soon arrived and left the motorcar at the gate, which was not open.

The doctor bade the chauffeur to wait for him. Then they quickly crossed the yard and entered the house. Frau Adele was sitting at Pierre's bedside.

Now, all at once, the doctor had plenty of time. He examined the child without haste, tried to make him talk, found words of kindly reassurance for the mother, and quietly created an atmosphere of businesslike confidence, which also had a soothing effect on Veraguth.

Pierre was uncooperative, silent, unfriendly, and distrustful. When the doctor palpated and pressed his abdomen, he made a scornful grimace, as though finding all this silly and useless.

"Poisoning seems excluded," said the doctor with deliberation, "and there's nothing wrong with his appendix. It's probably a plain spoiled stomach, and the best thing for that is to wait and see. No food. Don't give him anything today but a little tea if he's thirsty; this evening he can have a sip of Bordeaux. If he's

150)

better, give him tea and zwieback for breakfast. If he has pain, you can phone me."

Only when they left the room did Frau Veraguth begin to ask questions. But she obtained no further information.

"His stomach seems to be quite upset and the child is obviously sensitive and nervous. No trace of fever. You can take his temperature this evening. His pulse is a little weak. If he's not better, I'll come again tomorrow. I don't think it's anything serious."

He quickly said goodbye and was very much in a hurry again. Veraguth accompanied him to the motorcar.

"Can it last long?" he asked at the last moment.

The doctor gave a harsh laugh.

"I shouldn't have expected you to be such a worrier. The child is rather delicate and we all of us had plenty of spoiled stomachs as children. Good morning!"

Veraguth knew that he was not needed in the house and sauntered thoughtfully off into the fields. The doctor's succinct, austere manner had set his mind at rest, and now he was surprised that he should have been so agitated and fearful.

With a sense of relief, he strode along, drawing in the warm air of the deep-blue morning. It seemed to him that this was his farewell walk through these meadows and rows of fruit trees, and he felt passably happy and free at the thought. He wondered what had given him this new feeling that a decision had been made and a solution arrived at, and soon realized that it stemmed from his talk with Frau Adele that morning. That he had told her of his travel plans, that she had listened so calmly and made no attempt at resistance, that he had blocked off all possible loopholes and eva- sions between his decision and its execution, and that the immediate future now lay plain and clear before him—all this was a comfort to him, a source of peace and new self-confidence.

Without knowing where he was going, he had turned into the path he had taken a few weeks before with his friend Burkhardt. Only when the path began to climb did he notice where he was and remember his walk with Otto. He had intended in the autumn to paint the copse on the far side of the hill, the bench and the mysterious light-dark passage leading through the trees into the clear bluish valley framed like a picture in the distance; he had meant to seat Pierre on the bench, his bright boyish face resting softly in the subdued brown light of the forest.

Eagerly looking about him, he climbed, no longer aware of the noonday heat, and as he awaited the moment when he would see the edge of the woods over the crest of the hill, the day spent with Burkhardt came back to him, he remembered their conversation down to his friend's exact words and recalled the early summer green of the landscape, which had since then become much deeper and milder. He was overcome by a feeling he had not known in a long while and its unexpected recurrence reminded him sharply of his youth. For it seemed to him that since that walk in the woods with Otto a long long time had elapsed and that he himself had grown, had changed and gone forward to such a degree that he could not help looking back on himself as he was then with a certain ironic commiseration.

Surprised by this very youthful feeling, which twenty years earlier had been a part of his everyday life and now struck him as a rare enchantment, he looked back over the short summer and discovered something that had been unknown to him only yesterday. Recalling the days of two or three months past, he found himself transformed; today he found clarity and a feeling of certainty as to the road ahead, where only a short time ago there had been only darkness and perplexity. It was as though his life had become once more a limpid stream or river, driving resolutely in the direction assigned to it, whereas hitherto it had stagnated in the swampy lake of indecision. Now it became clear to him that his journey could not possibly lead him back here, that there was nothing more for him to do here than take his leave, perhaps with a bleeding heart, but no matter. His life was flowing again, driving resolutely toward freedom and the future. Though still unaware of it, he had inwardly renounced and cut himself off from the town and countryside, from Rosshalde and his wife.

He stopped still, breathing deeply, suffused and buoyed up by a wave of clarity. He thought of Pierre, and a keen wild pain pierced his whole being as the certainty came to him that he would have to travel this road to the end and part also with Pierre.

For a long while he stood there, his face twitching, and if what he felt was burning pain, still it was life and light, clarity and a sense of the future. This was what Otto Burkhardt had wanted of him. This was the hour for which his friend had been waiting. At last he had cut open the old abscesses he had so long feared to touch. A painful operation, bitterly painful, but now that he had abjured his cherished wishes, his unrest and disunity, the conflict and paralysis of his soul had died away with them. Daylight had risen around him, cruelly bright, beautiful, luminous daylight.

Deeply moved, he took the last steps to the hilltop and sat down on the shaded stone bench. A profound feeling of life poured through him as though his youth had returned, and in gratitude at his deliverance he thought of his distant friend, without whom he could never have found his way, without whom he would have perished in dull, sick captivity.

But it was not in his nature to meditate for long, or to sustain an extreme mood for long. Side by side with his feeling that he had recovered his health and his will, a new consciousness of energy and imperious personal power invaded his whole being.

He stood up, opened his eyes, and looked out avidly as though to take possession of his new picture. For a long while he peered through the forest shadow into the bright distant valley below. This was he wanted to paint, and he would not wait until fall. Here there was a challenging task, an enormous difficulty, a precious riddle to be solved: this wonderful passage through the woods had to be painted with love, with as much love and care as one of the fine old masters, an Altdorfer or a Dürer, would have put into it. Command of the light and its mystic rhythm would not be enough, every minute form would have to be given its full rights, to be as subtly appraised and modulated as the grasses in his mother's wonderful bouquets of wildflowers. The cool bright valley in the distance would have to be doubly thrust back, by the warm flowing light of the foreground and by the forest shade; it must be made to shine like a jewel from the depths of the picture, cool and sweet, strange and alluring.

L

He looked at his watch. It was time to go home. Today he did not wish to keep his wife waiting. But first he took out his little sketchbook and, standing in the noonday sun at the edge of the hill, he blocked in the picture with bold strokes, setting down the over-all perspective lines and the promising oval of the sparkling little scene in the distance.

Then he was late after all and, disregarding the heat, he ran down the steep sunny path. He thought of the painting materials he would need and decided to get up very early the next day in order to see the landscape in the first morning light. His heart rejoiced at the thought that once again a fine, challenging task awaited him.

"How is Pierre?" was his first question as he hurried into the house.

The child was tired and resting, Frau Adele answered; he seemed to have no pain and was lying patiently on his bed. She thought it best not to disturb him, he seemed strangely on edge, starting up whenever a door opened or there was any unexpected sound.

"Oh well," he nodded in reply, "I'll drop in on him later, toward evening perhaps. Forgive me for being a little late, I've been out. I shall be painting in the open for the next few days."

The luncheon was peaceful and quiet. Through the lowered blinds a green light filtered into the cool room, the windows were all open, and in the noonday silence the splashing of the little fountain in the yard could be heard.

"You'll be having to outfit yourself for India," said Albert. "Are you taking hunting equipment?"

"I don't think so, Burkhardt has everything. He'll tell me what to take. I believe my painting materials will have to be packed in sealed lead boxes."

"Will you wear a tropical helmet?"

"Of course. But I can buy one on the way."

When the meal was over and Albert had left the table, Frau Adele asked her husband to stay awhile. She sat down in her wicker chair by the window and he moved an armchair over beside her.

"When will you be leaving?" she asked.

"Oh, that depends entirely on Otto; whenever it suits him. About the end of September, I should think."

"So soon? I haven't had much time to think things over, I've been so busy with Pierre. But in connection with Pierre, I don't think you should ask too much of me."

"I agree with you, I was thinking about that this morning. I want you to feel perfectly free. I understand that it won't do for me to go traveling around the world and still expect to have a voice in your affairs here. You must do whatever you think right. There's no reason why you should have less freedom than I'm asking for myself."

"And what's to become of the house? I shouldn't like to stay here alone, it's too out-of-the-way and too big, and besides it's too full of memories that trouble me."

"I've already told you, go where you like. Rosshalde is yours, you know that, and before I leave I shall put it in writing, just in case."

Frau Adele had turned pale. She observed her husband's face with almost hostile attentiveness.

"You almost sound," she said in a tone of distress, "as though you were meaning never to come back."

He blinked thoughtfully and looked at the floor. "One never knows. I still have no idea how long I shall be away, and I hardly think that India is very healthy for a man my age."

She shook her head emphatically. "That's not what I meant. We can all die. I meant, have you any intention of coming back?"

He blinked and said nothing. At length he smiled feebly and rose. "Suppose we speak of that another time. Our last quarrel was about that question, a few years ago, do you remember? I don't want any more quarrels here in Rosshalde, least of all with you. I assume you still have the same ideas on the subject you did then. Or would you let me have Pierre today?"

Frau Veraguth shook her head in silence.

"Just as I thought," said her husband calmly. "We had better let these things rest. As I said, you can do what you like with the house. I attach no importance to keeping Rosshalde; if anyone offers you a good price for the place, why not sell it?"

"Then this is the end of Rosshalde," she said in a tone of deep bitterness, thinking of the early days, of Albert as a baby, and of all her old hopes and expectations.

Veraguth, who had already turned toward the door, turned around and said gently: "Don't take it so hard, child. Hold on to it if you like."

He went out and unchained the dog; the jubilant animal leapt around him barking as he crossed over to the studio. What was Rosshalde to him? It was one of the things he had left behind. Now for the first time he felt stronger than his wife. He had drawn a line. In his heart he had made his sacrifice, he had given up Pierre. Once that was done, his whole being looked only forward. For him Rosshalde was ended, ended like the many other miscarried hopes of those days, ended like his youth. There was no point in lamenting it.

He rang and Robert appeared.

"I shall be painting outside for a few days. Kindly have the small paint boxes and the sun shade ready for tomorrow. And wake me up at half past five."

"Certainly, Herr Veraguth."

"That's all. I suppose the weather will hold? What do you think?"

"I believe it will . . . But, excuse me, Herr Veraguth, there's something I should like to ask you."

"Well?"

"I beg your pardon, but I've heard you were going to India."

Veraguth laughed in surprise. "The news has traveled mighty fast. So Albert has been talking. Well, yes, I shall be going to India, and you can't very well come along, Robert, I'm sorry. There aren't any European servants out there. But you can always come back to me later if you like. Meanwhile, I'll find you another good position, and anyway your wages will be paid until New Year's."

"Thank you, Herr Veraguth, thank you very much. Perhaps you would give me your address. I shall want to write you. You see—it's not so easy to say—you see, I have a fiancée, Herr Veraguth."

"Oh, you have a fiancée?"

"Yes, Herr Veraguth, and if you let me go, I shall have to marry her. You see, I promised her I wouldn't take another position if I leave here."

"Well, then you'll be glad to get away. But I shall be sorry, Robert. What do you mean to do when you're married?"

"Well, she wants to open a cigar store with me."

"A cigar store? Robert, that's not for you."

"There's no harm in trying, Herr Veraguth. But begging your pardon . . . mightn't it be possible to continue in your service, Herr Veraguth?"

The painter clapped him on the shoulder. "Good Lord, man, what's going on here? You want to get married, you want to open an idiotic shop, and you want to stay with me too? Something seems to be wrong . . . I have the impression, Robert, that you're not exactly dead set on this marriage?"

"No, Herr Veraguth, begging your pardon, I'm not. My fiancée is a good worker, I won't deny it. But I'd rather stay with you. She has a sharp disposition and . . ."

"But, my dear fellow, why get married then? You're afraid of her! There isn't a child, I hope?"

"No, it's not that. But she leaves me no peace."

"In that case, Robert, give her a nice brooch, I'll contribute a taler. Give it to your fiancée and tell her to go find someone else for her cigar store. Tell her I said so. You ought to be ashamed! I'll give you a week's time. And then I'll want to know whether or not you're the kind of man that's afraid of a mere girl."

"All right, all right. I'll tell her . . ."

Veraguth stopped smiling. His eyes flashed angrily at the dismayed Robert: "You'll send that girl packing, Robert, or you and I are through. Humph—letting yourself be dragged to the altar! You may go now. See that this thing is settled in short order."

He filled a pipe and, taking with him a larger sketch-book and a bag full of charcoal, went out to the wooded hill.

Chapter Fourteen

FASTING DID NOT SEEM TO HELP. Pierre Veraguth lay huddled up in his bed, his cup of tea untouched. As far as possible, the others left him in peace, because he never answered when spoken to and recoiled irritably when anyone entered the room. Sometimes his mother sat by his bed, half mumbling, half singing words of tenderness and comfort. She felt strangely uneasy; it seemed to her that the little patient was stubbornly entrenching himself in a secret sorrow. He made no response to any question or plea or suggestion, stared gloomily into space, and showed no desire to sleep or play or drink or be read to. The doctor had come two days in succession; he had said little and recommended lukewarm compresses. A good deal of the time Pierre lay in a half sleep such as comes of fever, muttering incomprehensible words in a subdued, dreamlike delirium.

Veraguth had been out painting for several days. When he came home at dusk, he inquired after the boy. His wife asked him not to go into the sickroom because Pierre reacted so sensitively to the slightest disturbance and now he seemed to have dozed off. Since Frau Adele was not talkative and seemed since their recent conversation to feel ill-at-ease in his presence, he asked no further questions and went calmly off to his bath. He spent the evening in the warm, pleasant agitation that he always felt while preparing for a new piece of work. He had painted several studies and was planning to attack the painting itself the next day. With satisfaction he selected cardboards and canvases, repaired some stretchers that had come loose at the corners, gathered together brushes and painting materials of all kinds, and equipped himself as though for a short trip, even making ready his full tobacco pouch, pipe and lighter, in the manner of a tourist who is planning to climb a mountain in the morning and knows of no better way of spending the expectant hours before bedtime than to think lovingly of the day to come and to make ready every little thing he will need.

Later he settled himself with a glass of wine and looked over the evening mail. There was a joyful, affectionate letter from Burkhardt, who with the meticulousness of a good housewife had appended a list of everything Veraguth should take with him on the trip. With amusement Veraguth read through the whole list, which omitted neither woolen waist bands nor beach slippers, neither nightdress nor leggings. At the bottom Burkhardt had written in pencil: "I shall attend to everything else, including our cabins. Don't let anyone talk you into buying chemicals for seasickness, or Indian literature. I shall take care of all that."

Smiling, he turned to a large roll of cardboard containing some etchings which a young Düsseldorf painter had sent him with a respectful dedication. Today he found time for such things, he was in the mood, he examined the etchings with care and chose the best for his portfolios; he would give Albert the rest. He wrote the painter a friendly note.

Last, he opened his sketchbook and studied at length the many drawings he had made. He was not quite satisfied with any of them, he would try again next day, taking in a little more of the view, and if the picture was still not right, he would go on doing studies until he had it. In any case, he would work hard the next day, the rest would take care of itself. And this painting would be his farewell to Rosshalde; this was undoubtedly the most impressive and alluring piece of landscape in the region, and it would not be for nothing, he hoped, that he had time and again put off painting it. This was a subject that could not be disposed of in a dashing sketch, it demanded careful reflection. Later on in the tropics he would again relish the adventure of quick assaults on nature, with their difficulties, defeats, and victories.

He went to bed early and slept soundly until Robert awakened him. Then he arose in joyful haste, shivering

in the sharp morning air, drank a bowl of coffee standing up, meanwhile urging haste upon Robert, who was
to carry his canvas, camp chair, and paintbox. A little
while later he left the house and disappeared, followed
by Robert, into the morning-pale meadows. He had
meant to drop into the kitchen to ask if Pierre had had
a quiet night, but found the house closed up and no one
awake.

Frau Adele had sat up a part of the night with the
child, who seemed slightly feverish. She had listened to
his incoherent mumbling, felt his pulse, and straightened his bed. When she said good night and kissed him,
he opened his eyes and looked into her face but did not
answer. The night was quiet.

Pierre was awake when she entered his room in the
morning. He wanted no breakfast but asked for a picture book. His mother went to get one. She wedged
another pillow under his head, pushed aside the window curtains, and put the book into Pierre's hands; it
was open to a picture he was especially fond of,
showing a large, gleaming, golden-yellow Lady Sun.

He lifted the book to his face, the bright joyful
morning light fell on the page. But instantly a dark
shadow of pain and disappointment crossed his sensitive face.

"Ugh, it hurts!" he cried out in torment and let the
book drop.

She caught it and held it up to his eyes again. "But it's Lady Sun whom you love so dearly," she pleaded.

He held his hands before his eyes. "No, take it away. It's so disgustingly yellow!"

With a sigh she removed the book. What could be the matter with the child! She knew his moods and sensibilities, but he had never been like this.

"I have an idea," she said hopefully. "Suppose I bring you a lovely cup of tea and you can put sugar in it and have a nice piece of zwieback to go with it."

"I don't want it!"

"Just try. It will do you good, you'll see."

He gave her a tortured, furious look. "But I don't want it!"

She left the room and stayed away for some time. He blinked at the light, it seemed unusually glaring and hurt him. He turned away. Was there never again to be any comfort, any bit of pleasure, any little joy for him? Whimpering, he buried his face in his pillow and bit angrily into the soft, insipid-tasting linen. This was a remote echo of his earliest childhood. When as a very little boy he had been put to bed and sleep did not come quickly, it had been his habit to bite into his pillow and to chew it rhythmically until he grew tired and fell asleep. Now he did so again and slowly worked himself into a silent stupor that made him feel better. Then he lay still.

(167

His mother came back an hour later. She bent over him and said: "Well now, is Pierre going to be a good boy again? You were very naughty before and Mama was sad."

In former times this had been strong medicine which he seldom resisted. As she said the words now, she was almost afraid he would take them too much to heart and burst into tears. But he seemed to pay no attention, and when she asked him with a note of severity: "You do know you were naughty before?" his lip curled almost scornfully and he looked at her with utter indifference.

Just then the doctor arrived.

"Has he vomited again? No? Fine. And he's had a good night? What did he have for breakfast?"

When he raised the child in his bed and turned his face toward the window, Pierre winced with pain and closed his eyes. The doctor was struck by the intense look of revulsion and misery in the child's face.

"Is he also sensitive to sounds?" he asked Frau Adele in a whisper.

"Yes," she said softly. "We can't play the piano any more, it was driving him to despair."

The doctor nodded and half closed the curtains. Then he lifted the child out of bed, listened to his heart, and tapped the ligaments under his kneecaps with a little hammer.

"That will do," he said in a friendly tone. "We won't bother you any more, my boy."

He carefully put him back into bed, took his hand, and smiled at him.

"May I drop in on you for a moment?" he asked Frau Veraguth with a note of gallantry, and she led him into her sitting room.

"Now tell me a little more about your boy," he said encouragingly. "It seems to me that he's very nervous; we shall have to take good care of him for a while, you and I. His upset stomach is nothing. He must absolutely start eating again. Good things that will build up his strength: eggs, bouillon, fresh cream. Try him on egg yolks. If he prefers them sweet, beat them up in a cup with sugar. And now tell me, have you noticed anything else?"

Alarmed and yet reassured by his friendly, confident tone, she reported. Most of all she had been frightened by Pierre's indifference, it was as though he didn't love anyone any more. It was all the same to him whether one spoke kindly to him or scolded him. She told the doctor about the picture book and he nodded.

"Give him his way," he said, rising. "He's sick and for the moment he can't help behaving badly. Let him rest as much as possible. If he has a headache, you can put on cold compresses. And in the evening let him bathe as

(169

long as possible in lukewarm water, that will make him sleep."

He took his leave and would not let her see him down the stairs. "Make sure that he eats something today," he said as he was going.

Down below, he passed through the open kitchen door and asked for Veraguth's servant.

"Call Robert over," the cook ordered the maid. "He must be in the studio."

"Never mind," said the doctor. "I'll go over myself. No, don't bother, I know the way."

He left the kitchen with a quip. Then suddenly grave and thoughtful, he walked slowly down the path under the chestnut trees.

Frau Veraguth thought over every word the doctor had said and she could not quite make up her mind. Apparently he took Pierre's illness more seriously than before, but he had actually said nothing alarming, and he had been so calm and matter-of-fact it was hard to think there was any serious danger. It seemed to be a state of weakness and nervousness that would pass with patience and good care.

She went to the music room and locked the piano for fear that Albert might forget himself and start playing. And she wondered to which room she might move the piano if this should go on for a long time.

Every few minutes she went to see how Pierre was, opened his door cautiously and listened to see if he was sleeping or moaning. Each time he was lying awake, looking apathetically straight ahead, and sadly she went away. She would rather have cared for him in danger and pain than see him lying there so closed in, so gloomy and indifferent; it seemed to her that the two of them were separated by a strange dream space, a dreadful, powerful barrier that her love and care were unable to break through. A treacherous, hateful enemy lay in ambush; his nature and evil purposes were unknown to her and she had no weapons against him. Perhaps the child was coming down with scarlet fever or some other children's disease.

Troubled, she rested awhile in her room. A bunch of spiraea struck her eye. She bent over the round mahogany table, the red-brown wood shone deep and warm under the openwork cloth. She closed her eyes and buried her face in the soft summery blossoms, whose sweet pungent smell, when she breathed it deeply, had a strangely bitter undertone.

As she straightened up, slightly stupefied, and let her eyes roam idly over the flowers, the table, the room, a wave of bitter sadness rose up in her. Her mind grown suddenly alert, she looked about the room and along the walls, and all at once the carpet, the table with the

M

flowers on it, the clock, and the pictures looked strange and unrelated to one another; she saw the carpet rolled up, the pictures packed, and everything loaded into a van that would carry all these objects, now without home or soul, away to a new, unknown, indifferent place. She saw Rosshalde standing empty with closed doors and windows, and she felt forsakenness and the sadness of parting staring at her from the flower beds of the garden.

Only for a few moments at a time. The feeling came and went like a low but urgent cry from the darkness, like a briefly projected fragmentary image of the future. And the thought rose clearly to her consciousness from the blind realm of the emotions that she would soon be homeless with her Albert and with little sick Pierre, her husband would leave her, and the bleak forlorn coldness of the loveless years would lie on her soul forever. She would live for her children, but she would never again find the beautiful life of her own which she had hoped Veraguth would give her and the secret claim to which she had continued to treasure and cherish until yesterday and today. For that it was too late. And her disenchanted knowledge chilled her heart.

But her robust nature rose at once to the defensive. Days of anxiety and uncertainty lay ahead of her, Pierre was sick, and Albert's vacation would soon be at an end. It wouldn't do, it just wouldn't do for her to weaken now and listen to subterranean voices. First Pierre must be well again and Albert back at school and Veraguth in India, then she would see, then there would still be plenty of time to rebel against her fate and cry her eyes out. Now it was pointless, she mustn't, it was out of the question.

She put the vase of spiraea out on the windowsill. She went to her bedroom, poured cologne on her handkerchief and wiped her forehead, examined her careful severe coiffure in the mirror, and went with calm, measured steps to the kitchen to make Pierre something to eat.

Then she went to the child's room, sat him up straight, disregarded his gestures of protest, and carefully and unsmilingly fed him the egg yolk. She wiped his mouth, kissed him on the forehead, smoothed his bed, and told him to be a good child now and go to sleep.

When Albert came home from a walk, she led him out to the veranda, where the taut brown-and-white-striped awnings were flapping in the summer breeze.

"The doctor has been here again," she told him. "He says there's something wrong with Pierre's nerves and he must have as much quiet as possible. I'm sorry for your sake, but for the present there can't be any piano

(173

playing in the house. I know it's hard for you, my boy. Perhaps it would be a good idea for you to go away for a few days while the weather is good, to the mountains or to Munich? Papa would certainly have no objection."

"Thank you, Mama, you're very kind. Maybe I'll go off for a day, but no more. You'd have no one to stay with you while Pierre is in bed. And besides, I ought to start on my schoolwork, I've been loafing up to now. If only Pierre gets well soon!"

"That's a good boy, Albert. It's really not an easy time for me, and I'm very glad to have you here. And you've been getting along better with Papa lately, haven't you?"

"Oh yes, ever since he decided to go away. Besides, I see him so little. He paints all day. You know, sometimes I feel sorry that I've been nasty to him—oh, of course he has tortured me, but there's something about him that always impresses me. He's dreadfully one-sided, he doesn't know much about music, but he is a great artist and he's got his life work. That's what impresses me so. He doesn't get anything out of his fame, and not much out of his money either: that's not what he works for."

Frowning, he groped for words. But he was unable to express himself as he wished, although it was a very definite feeling. His mother smiled and stroked back his hair.

174)

"Shall we read French together again this evening?" she asked coaxingly.

He nodded and then he too smiled. At that moment it struck her as unbelievably absurd that only a little while before she could have yearned for any better lot than to live for her sons.

Chapter Fifteen

S HORTLY BEFORE NOON, Robert went out to his master at the edge of the woods to help him carry home his painting materials. Veraguth had finished a new study, which he wished to carry himself. Now he knew exactly how the picture had to be and felt confident of mastering it in a few days.

"We'll be coming out again tomorrow morning," he cried joyfully, blinking with tired eyes at the dazzling noonday world.

Robert unbuttoned his jacket with deliberation and took a piece of paper from his inside pocket. It was a rather rumpled envelope with no address.

"This is for you."

"From whom?"

"From the doctor. He came looking for you at ten o'clock, but I told him I couldn't call you away from your work."

"You did well. And now forward march!"

The servant went ahead with knapsack, camp chair, and easel. Veraguth stayed behind and, suspecting bad news, opened the envelope. It contained only the doctor's visiting card with a message scribbled hastily and none too legibly in pencil: "Please come to see me this afternoon, I should like to speak to you about Pierre. His indisposition is not as insignificant as I thought preferable to tell your wife. Don't torment yourself with useless worry until we have had a chance to talk."

He fought down the terror that threatened to take his breath away, forced himself to keep calm, and read the note through again attentively. "Not as insignificant as I thought preferable to tell your wife!" That was the enemy. His wife was hardly the delicate, high-strung type that had to be shielded from every unpleasantness. In other words, it was bad, it was dangerous, Pierre might die. On the other hand, he spoke of an "indisposition"; that sounded so harmless. And then "useless worry"! No, it couldn't be as bad as all that. Something contagious perhaps, a children's disease. Perhaps the doctor wanted to isolate him, to put him in a hospital.

He grew calmer as he thought it over. Slowly he made his way home, down the hill and through the hot fields. In any case, he would do as the doctor wished and not let his wife notice anything.

But on his return he was seized with impatience. Without even taking time to put his picture away and wash, he ran to the manor house, leaned the wet painting against the wall in the stairwell, and quietly entered Pierre's room. His wife was there.

He bent down over the boy and kissed his hair.

"Good morning, Pierre. How are you feeling?"

Pierre smiled feebly. An instant later, he began to sniff, his nostrils trembled, and he cried out: "No, no, go away! You smell so bad!"

Veraguth stepped back obediently. "It's only turpentine, my boy. Papa hasn't washed yet because he was in a hurry to see you. Now I'll go and change and I'll be right back. All right?"

He left the house, picking up the canvas on his way; the child's plaintive voice still rang in his ears.

At table he asked what the doctor had said and was pleased to hear that Pierre had eaten and had not vomited again. Still, he felt agitated and uneasy and labored to keep up a conversation with Albert.

After lunch he sat for half an hour with Pierre, who lay quiet except for rare moments when he clutched his forehead as in pain. With loving anxiety Veraguth observed his narrow mouth, which looked languid and slack, and the handsome bright forehead, which now bore a faint vertical crease, a sickly but softly childlike crease that would go away when Pierre was well again. And the child must get well—even though he would then suffer doubly to go away and leave him. He must live to grow in his bright, delicate, boyish beauty and breathe like a flower in the sun, even if his father had bidden him farewell and were never to see him again. He must get well and become a beautiful, radiant man

in whom what was purest and most sensitive in his
father lived on.

As he sat by the child's bedside, Veraguth had a foreboding of all the bitterness he would have to taste before all this lay behind him. His lips quivered and his
heart shrank away from the thorn, but deep beneath all
his suffering and fear he felt his decision, hard and
indestructible. There it was; pain and suffering could
no longer shake it. But it still behooved him to live
through this last phase, to sidestep no suffering, to
drain the cup to the last drop, for in these last few days
he had seen clearly that his road to life must lead
through this dark gate. If he were cowardly now, if he
fled and recoiled from suffering, he would be taking
muck and poison with him when he left and would
never attain the pure sacred freedom for which he
yearned and for which he was willing to incur every
torment.

Well, first of all he must speak to the doctor. He
stood up with an affectionate nod to Pierre, and left the
room. The idea crossed his mind of letting Albert drive
him in, and for the first time that summer he went to
his room. He knocked firmly on the door.

"Come in!"

Albert sat by the window, reading. He jumped up in
surprise and went toward his father.

"I have a little favor to ask of you, Albert. Could you

drive me to town?—Yes? That's fine. Then would you run down and help harness the horses, I'm rather in a hurry. Cigarette?"

"Yes, thank you. I'll attend to the horses right away."

Soon they were in the carriage. Albert sat on the box and drove. At a street corner in town, Veraguth bade him stop and took his leave with a few words of appreciation.

"Thank you, Albert. You're doing very well, you've got these nags well in hand now. Well, goodbye, I'll be walking home later on."

He strode quickly down the hot city street. The doctor lived in a quiet, fashionable neighborhood. At that time of day there was hardly a soul abroad. A water wagon drove along sleepily; two little boys ran behind it, held their hands out into the light rain of the sprinkler and, laughing, splashed each other's overheated faces. From an open, ground-floor window, the sound of listless piano practicing could be heard. Veraguth had always felt a deep dislike of lifeless city streets, especially in the summer; they reminded him of his younger days, when he had lived in such streets in dismal cheap rooms, opening out onto hallways redolent of cooking and coffee, and offering a view of attic windows, carpet-beating racks, and ridiculously small gardens without charm.

In the anteroom, amid large, gold-framed pictures

and thick carpets, a discreet doctor-smell gathered him
in and a young girl in a long, snow-white nurse's apron
took his card. First she showed him into the waiting
room, where several women and a young man sat quiet
and subdued in plush armchairs, staring at magazines;
then at his request she took him to another room, in
which innumerable issues of a medical journal lay
piled. He had scarcely had time to look around when
the girl came back and led him to the doctor's office.

There Veraguth sat in a large leather armchair, in an
atmosphere of efficiency and glistening cleanliness.
Facing him at the desk sat the doctor, a short man of
dignified bearing; there was no sound in the high-
ceilinged room except for the sharp rhythmic ticking
of a shining little clock, all glass and brass.

"Yes, my friend, I'm not very happy about your boy.
Haven't you been struck for some time by certain ab-
normalities, headaches, fatigue, no desire to play, and
so on? —Only very recently? And has he been so sensitive for very long? To noise and bright light? To
smells? —I see. He disliked the smell of paint in your
studio! Yes, that fits in."

He asked a good many questions and Veraguth
answered. Though slightly numb, he was anxiously attentive and felt a secret admiration for the doctor's
considerately polite, flawlessly precise manner of
speaking.

Then the questions came slowly and singly, and at length there was a long pause, silence hovered in midair like a cloud, broken only by the sharp, high-pitched ticking of the pretty little clock.

Veraguth wiped the perspiration from his forehead. He felt that it was time for him to learn the truth, and conscious of the doctor's stony silence, he was overcome by painful, paralyzing fear. He squirmed as though his shirt collar were choking him, and at last he blurted out: "Is it as bad as all that?"

Raising his sallow, overworked face, the doctor gave him a wan glance and nodded. "Yes, I'm sorry to say. It's bad, Herr Veraguth."

The doctor did not avert his eyes. Attentively waiting, he saw the painter turn pale and let his hands drop. He saw the lips sag and tremble slightly and the lids droop over the eyes as in a faint. And then he saw the painter's mouth recover its firmness and his eyes kindle with fresh will. Only the deep pallor remained. He saw that the painter was ready to listen.

"What is it, Doctor? You don't have to spare me. Speak up. —You don't think Pierre is going to die?"

The doctor moved his chair a little closer. He spoke very softly, but sharply and distinctly. "That's a question no one can answer. But if I'm not greatly mistaken, your little boy is dangerously ill."

Veraguth looked into his eyes. "Is he going to die? I

want to know if you think he's going to die. Do you understand—I want to know."

Unconsciously, the painter had stood up and stepped forward almost menacingly. The doctor put his hand on his arm; Veraguth gave a start and immediately sank back into his chair as though ashamed.

"There's no sense in talking like that," the doctor began. "The decision between life and death doesn't rest with us. Every day we physicians meet with surprises. As long as a patient has breath, we have hope for him. You know that. Or where would we be?"

Veraguth nodded patiently and merely asked: "What is it, then?"

The doctor coughed slightly.

"If I'm not mistaken, it's meningitis."

Veraguth sat very still and softly repeated the word. Then he stood up and held out his hand to the doctor. "So it's meningitis," he said, speaking very slowly and cautiously because his lips were trembling as though it was very cold. "Is that ever curable?"

"Everything is curable, Herr Veraguth. One man takes to his bed with a toothache and dies in a few days, another has all the symptoms of the worst disease and gets well."

"Yes, yes. And gets well! I'll go now, Herr Doktor. You've been to a lot of trouble on my account. In other words, meningitis isn't curable?"

"My dear Herr . . ."

"Forgive me. Perhaps you have taken care of other children with this meni . . . with this disease? Yes? You see! . . . Are those children still alive?"

The doctor was silent.

"Are two of them still alive? Or one?"

There was no answer.

As though vexed, the doctor had turned toward his desk and opened a drawer.

"You musn't give up like that!" he said in a changed tone. "Whether your child will get well, we don't know. He is in danger, and we've got to help him as best we can. We must all of us help him, do you understand, and you too. I need you. —I'll be out to the house again this evening. In any case, I'm giving you this sleeping powder, perhaps you can use it yourself. And now listen to me: the child must have absolute quiet and the most nourishing food. That's the main thing. Will you keep that in mind?"

"Of course. I won't forget."

"If he has pain or is very restless, lukewarm baths or compresses help. Have you an ice bag? I'll bring you one. You do have ice out there? Good. —We shall go on hoping, Herr Veraguth. It won't do for any of us to lose heart now, we've all got to be at our posts. Agreed?"

Veraguth replied with a gesture that inspired confidence in the doctor. The doctor saw him to the door.

"Would you like to take my carriage? I won't need it until five."

"No, thank you. I'll walk."

He went down the street, which was as deserted as before. The joyless piano practicing was still pouring from the open window. He looked at his watch. Only half an hour had passed. Slowly he went on, street after street, by a circuitous route that took him through half the city. He dreaded to leave it. Here in this poor, stupid heap of houses, medicine-smell and sickness, affliction and fear and death were at home, a hundred dismal languishing streets helped to bear every burden, one was not alone. But out there, it seemed to him, under the trees and clear sky, amid the singing of scythes and the chirping of crickets, the thought of all that must be much more terrible, more meaningless, more desperate.

It was evening when he arrived home, dusty and dead tired. The doctor had called, but Frau Adele was calm and seemed to know nothing.

At dinner Veraguth spoke about horses with Albert. At every turn he thought of something to say, and Albert joined in. They saw that Papa was very tired, nothing more. But he kept thinking with almost scornful bitterness: I could have death in my eyes, they would never notice! This is my wife and this is my son! And Pierre is dying! And these thoughts circled dismally through his head while his wooden tongue formed words that were of no interest to anyone. But then came a new thought: So much the better! This way I shall drink my suffering to the last bitter drop. I shall sit here dissembling, and see my poor little boy die. And if I'm still alive after that, there will be nothing more to bind me, nothing more that can hurt me; then I will go and never lie again as long as I live, never again believe in a love, never again procrastinate and be cowardly . . . Then I will live and act and go forward, there will be no peace and no inertia.

With dark delight he felt the suffering burn in his heart, wild and unbearable, but pure and great, a feeling such as he had never known before, and in the presence of the divine flame he saw his small, dismal, disingenuous and misshapen life dwindle into insignificance, unworthy of so much as a thought or even of blame.

In that frame of mind, he sat for an hour in the child's half-darkened sickroom and spent a burning sleepless night in his bed, giving himself with fervor to his devouring grief, desiring nothing and hoping for nothing, as though wishing to be consumed by this fire and burned clean down to the last quivering fiber. He understood that this had to be, that he must relinquish his dearest and best and purest possession, and see it die.

Chapter Sixteen

PIERRE WAS SUFFERING and his father sat with him almost all day. The child had a constant head-ache; he breathed rapidly, and every breath was a brief, anguished moan. At times his little thin body was shaken with brief tremors or stiffened and arched. Then for a long while he lay perfectly still, and at length he was overcome by a convulsive yawning. Then he slept for an hour, and when he woke, the same regular, plaintive sigh resumed with every breath.

He did not hear what was said to him and when they raised him almost by force and put food into his mouth, he ate it with mechanical indifference. The curtains were closed tight and in the dim light Veraguth sat for a long while bent watchfully over the child, observing with freezing heart how one delicate sweet trait after another vanished from the child's lovely familiar face and was gone. What remained was a pale, prematurely aged face, a gruesome mask with simplified features, in which nothing could be read but pain and disgust and profound horror.

At times, when the child dozed off, the father saw the disfigured face soften and recover a trace of its lost

N

charm, and then he stared fixedly, with all the thirsting fervor of his love, once again and then again to imprint this dying loveliness on his mind. Then it seemed to him that he had never in all his life known what love was, never until these watchful moments.

For a long time Frau Adele had suspected nothing; Veraguth's tenseness and strange remoteness had struck her only gradually and in the end aroused her suspicions, but it was days before she gained an intimation of the truth. One evening as he was leaving Pierre's room she took him aside and said brusquely, in an offended, bitter tone: "Well, what *is* the matter with Pierre? What is it? I see that you know something."

He looked at her as though from far off, and said with dry lips: "I don't know, child. He's very sick. Can't you see that?"

"I do see. And I want to know what it is! You treat him almost as if he were dying—you and the doctor. What has he told you?"

"He told me it was bad and that we must take very good care of him. It's some sort of inflammation in his poor little head. We'll ask the doctor to tell us more tomorrow."

She leaned against the bookcase, reaching up with one hand to grasp the folds of the green curtain above her. She said nothing and he stood there patiently; his face was gray and his eyes looked inflamed. His hands

were trembling slightly, but he kept control of himself
and on his face there was a sort of smile, a strange
shadow of resignation, patience, and politeness.

Slowly she came over to him. She put her hand on
his arm and seemed unsteady in the knees. Very softly
she whispered: "Do you think he's going to die?"

Veraguth still had the weak foolish smile on his lips,
but quick little tears were running down his face. He
only nodded feebly, and when she slumped down and
lost her hold, he lifted her up and helped her to a chair.

"We can't know for sure," he said slowly and awkwardly, as though repeating with disgust an old lesson
with which he had long ago lost patience. "We mustn't
lose heart."

"We mustn't lose heart," he repeated mechanically
after a time, when her strength had returned and she
was sitting up straight again.

"Yes," she said. "Yes, you're right." And again after a
pause: "It can't be! It can't be!"

And suddenly she stood up, there was life in her eyes
and her face was full of understanding and grief.
"You're not coming back, are you?" she said aloud. "I
know. You're going to leave us."

He saw clearly that this was a moment which per-
mitted of no falsehood. And so he said quickly and
tonelessly: "Yes."

She rocked her head as though she had to think very

hard and was unable to take it all in. But what she now said was not a product of reflection; it flowed unconsciously from the black, hopeless affliction of the moment, from weariness and discouragement, and most of all from an obscure need to make amends for something and to do a kindness to someone still accessible to kindness.

"That's what I thought," she said. "But listen to me, Johann. Pierre mustn't die. Everything mustn't collapse now all at once! And do you know . . . there's something else I want to tell you: if he gets well, you may have him. Do you hear me? He shall stay with you."

Veraguth did not understand immediately. Only gradually did he grasp what she had said and realize that what they had fought over, what had made him hesitate and suffer for years, had been granted him now that it was too late.

It struck him as unspeakably absurd, not only that he should now suddenly have what had so long been denied him, but even more, that Pierre should become his at the very moment when he was doomed to die. Now, to him, the child would die doubly! It was insane, it was ridiculous! It was so grotesque and absurd that he was almost on the point of bursting into bitter laughter.

But, beyond a doubt, she meant it seriously. It was clear that she did not fully believe Pierre must die. It was a kindness, it was an enormous sacrifice which some obscure good impulse drove her to make in the painful confusion of the moment. He saw how she was suffering, how pale she was, and what an effort it cost her to stand on her feet. He must not show that he took her sacrifice, her strange belated generosity, as a deadly mockery.

Already she was waiting uneasily for a word from him. Why didn't he say something? Didn't he believe her? Or had he become so estranged that he was unwilling to accept anything from her, not even this, the greatest sacrifice she could make him?

Her face began to tremble with disappointment, and then at last he regained control of himself. He took her hand, bent over, touched it with his cool lips, and said: "Thank you."

Then an idea came to him and in a warmer tone he added: "But now I want to help take care of Pierre. Let me sit up with him at night."

"We shall take turns," she said firmly.

That night Pierre was very quiet. On the table a little night lamp was left burning; its feeble light did not fill the room but lost itself halfway to the door in a brown twilight. For a long while Veraguth listened to the boy's breathing, then he lay down on the narrow divan that he had had moved into the room.

At about two in the morning Frau Adele awoke,

struck a light, and arose. She threw on her dressing
gown and, holding a candle, went to Pierre's room. She
found everything quiet. Pierre's eyelashes flickered
slightly as the light grazed his face, but he did not
awaken. And on the divan her husband lay asleep, fully
dressed and half curled up.

She let the light fall on his face as well, and stood
over him for a few minutes. And she saw his face shorn
of pretense, with all its wrinkles and gray hair, its
sagging cheeks and sunken eyes.

"He too has grown old," she thought with a feeling of
mingled pity and satisfaction, and felt tempted to
stroke the disheveled hair. But she did not. She left the
room without a sound. When she came back in the
morning, he had long been sitting awake and attentive
at Pierre's bedside. His mouth and the glance with
which he greeted her were again firm with the resolu-
tion and secret strength which for some days now had
enveloped him like armor.

For Pierre, a bad day was beginning. He slept a good
deal of the time with fixed open eyes until a new wave
of pain awakened him. He tossed furiously about in his
bed, clenched his little fists, and pressed them into his
eyes; his face was at times deathly white, at times
flaming red. And then he began to scream in helpless
rage at the intolerable torment; he screamed so long

and so pitifully that his father, pale and crushed, had to leave the room because he could bear it no longer.

He sent for the doctor, who came twice that day and in the evening brought a nurse with him. A little later Pierre lost consciousness, the nurse was sent to bed, and father and mother watched through the night with the feeling that the end could not be far off. The child did not stir and his breathing was irregular but strong.

But Veraguth and his wife both thought of the time when Albert had been seriously ill and they had cared for him together. And they both felt that important experiences cannot be repeated. Gently and rather wearily, they spoke to one another in whispers across the sickbed, but not a word of the past, of Albert's illness. The similarity in the situations struck them as ghostlike, they themselves had changed, they were no longer the same persons who then as now had watched and suffered together, bowed over a deathly sick child.

Meanwhile, Albert, oppressed by the unspoken anxiety and creeping dread in the house, had been unable to sleep. In the middle of the night he tiptoed half dressed to the door, came in, and asked in an excited whisper whether there was something he could do to help.

"Thank you," said Veraguth, "but there's nothing to do. Go to bed and keep your health."

But when Albert had gone, he said to his wife: "Go in with him for a while and comfort him."

She gladly complied and she felt that it had been kind of him to think of it.

Not until morning did she incline to her husband's pleas and go to bed. At daybreak the nurse appeared and relieved him. There had been no change in Pierre.

Irresolutely Veraguth crossed the park, he had no desire to sleep. But his burning eyes and a slack, stifled feeling in his skin warned him that he had better. He bathed in the lake and asked Robert to make coffee. Then in the studio he looked at his study of the woods. The painting was brisk and fresh, but it was not really what he had been aiming at, and now it was all up with his projected picture and he would never paint again in Rosshalde.

Chapter Seventeen

F OR SOME DAYS there had been no change in Pierre.
Once or twice a day he would be taken with
spasms and onslaughts of pain; the rest of the time he
lay with senses dimmed in a half sleep. The warm
weather had worn itself out in a series of storms, and
under a steady drizzle the garden and the world lost
their rich summer radiance.

At last Veraguth had spent a night in his own bed
and slept. The last few days he had gone about in feverish weariness, and now as he was dressing with the
window open, he suddenly became aware of the dismal
cold. He leaned out the window and, shivering slightly,
breathed in the rainy air of the lightless morning.
There was a smell of wet earth and of approaching fall,
and he, who ordinarily was keenly alive to the signs of
the seasons, reflected with surprise that this summer
had vanished for him almost without trace, as though
unperceived. It seemed to him that he had spent not
days and nights but whole months in Pierre's sickroom.

He threw on his raincoat and went over to the house.
Informed that the child had wakened early but had
dropped off to sleep again an hour before, he kept

Albert company at breakfast. Albert took Pierre's illness very much to heart and, though he tried not to show it, suffered from the subdued hospital atmosphere, the dejection and anxiety about him.

When Albert had gone to his room to busy himself with his schoolwork, Veraguth went in to see Pierre, who was still asleep, and took his place by the child's bedside. Sometimes, in recent days, he had wished that the end would come quickly, if only for the sake of the child, who had not spoken a word in heaven knows how long and who looked so exhausted and aged, as though he himself knew he was beyond help. Yet Veraguth was unwilling to miss an hour, he clung to his post at the sickbed with jealous passion. Oh, how often little Pierre had come to him and found him tired or indifferent, deep in his work or lost in care, how often his mind had been far away as he held this thin little hand in his and he had scarcely listened to the child's words, each one of which had now become an inestimable treasure. That could never be made good. But now that the poor child lay in torment, facing death alone with his spoiled, defenseless little heart, now that he was condemned to experience in the space of a few days all the numbing pain, all the anguish of despair with which illness, weakness, growing older, and the approach of death terrify and oppress a human heart, now he wished to be with him always and always. He must not be absent and missed if ever a moment came when the child should want him, when he might be of some little help to him or show him a little love.

And lo and behold, that morning he was rewarded. That morning Pierre opened his eyes, smiled at him, and said in a weak, tender voice: "Papa!"

The painter's heart beat stormily when at last he heard the voice which he had missed so long, which had become so thin and feeble, calling out to him and acknowledging him. It had been so long since he had heard that voice otherwise than moaning and muttering wretchedly in dull suffering, that he was terror-stricken with joy.

"Pierre, my darling!"

He bent down tenderly and kissed the smiling lips. Pierre looked fresher and happier than he had ever hoped to see him again, his eyes were clear and alert, the deep crease between the brows had almost disappeared.

"Are you feeling better, my angel?"

The little boy smiled and looked at him as though in surprise. His father held out his hand and into it the child put his little hand, which had never been very strong and was now so tiny and white and tired.

"Now you'll have your breakfast right away, and then I shall tell you stories."

"Oh yes, about Mr. Larkspur and the birds," said

Pierre, and to his father it seemed a miracle that he should speak and smile and belong to him again.

He brought him his breakfast. Pierre ate willingly and even let himself be cajoled into a second egg. Then he asked for his favorite picture book. His father cautiously thrust one of the curtains aside, admitting the pale light of the rainy day, and Pierre tried to sit up and look at pictures. The effort seemed to give him no pain, he studied several pages attentively and greeted the beloved pictures with little cries of joy. Then he grew tired from sitting and his eyes began to hurt a little. He let his father lay him down again and asked him to read some of the verses, especially the one about Creeping Cucumber who goes to see Apothecary Mistletoe:

> *Apothecary Mistletoe,*
> *Oh, help me with your ointments!*
> *I cannot come, I cannot go,*
> *I ache in all my jointments!*

Veraguth was at pains to read as gaily and waggishly as possible, and Pierre smiled gratefully. But the verses seemed to have lost their old force, as though Pierre had grown years older since last hearing them. The pictures and verses kindled memories of many bright, laughing days, but the old joy and lightheartedness could not come again, and already, without knowing why, Pierre looked back into his childhood, which had still been reality days and weeks ago, with the yearning and sadness of an adult. He was no longer a child. He was an invalid from whom the world of reality had slipped away and whose soul, grown clairvoyant, already sensed the presence of lurking death on all sides.

Nevertheless, that morning was full of light and happiness after all the terrible days. Pierre was quiet and thankful and Veraguth against his will felt time and again the touch of hope. Wasn't it possible that the child would be spared after all? And then he would belong to him; to him alone!

The doctor came and stayed a long while at Pierre's bedside but did not torment him by asking him questions or examining him. It was only then that Frau Adele, who had shared the last night watch with the nurse, appeared. She was overwhelmed by the unexpected improvement, she held Pierre's hands so hard that it hurt him, and struggled to hold back the tears of relief that welled in her eyes. Albert, too, was allowed in for a little while.

"It's a miracle," said Veraguth to the doctor. "Aren't you surprised?"

The doctor nodded and gave a friendly smile. He did not say no, but neither did he show any great enthusiasm. At once the painter was assailed by suspicion. He watched the doctor closely and saw that, even as his face smiled, the cold concentration and restrained

O·

anxiety were undiminished in his eyes. Afterward, he listened through the crack in the door to the doctor's conversation with the nurse, and although he could not understand a word, there seemed to be nothing but danger in the severe, earnest tone of his whispers.

At length he saw him to his carriage and asked at the last minute: "I gather you don't think much of this improvement?"

The ugly, self-controlled face turned back to him: "Be glad that he has a few good hours, the poor little tyke! Let's hope that it lasts a long while."

There was no sign of hope to be read in his shrewd eyes.

Quickly, so as not to lose a moment, he returned to the sickroom. Frau Adele was telling the story of Sleeping Beauty; he sat down beside her and watched Pierre's features follow the story.

"Shall I tell you another?" Frau Adele asked.

"No," he said rather wearily. "Later."

She went to give orders in the kitchen and Veraguth took the boy's hand. They were both silent but from time to time Pierre looked up with a faint smile, as though glad that his father was with him.

"You're much better now," Veraguth said tenderly.

Pierre flushed slightly, his fingers moved playfully in his father's hand. "You love me, Papa, don't you?"

"Of course I love you, sweetheart. You're my dear

boy, and when you're well again we shall always be together."

"Oh yes, Papa . . . Once I was in the garden and I was all alone, and none of you loved me any more. You must all love me and you must help me when it hurts again. Oh, it hurt so badly!"

His eyes were half closed and he spoke so softly that Veraguth had to lean close to his mouth to understand him.

"You must help me. I'll be good, always, you mustn't scold me. You won't ever scold me, will you? And you must tell Albert, too."

His eyelids quivered and opened, but the look in his eyes was dark and his pupils were much too large.

"Sleep, child, sleep. You're tired. Sleep, sleep, sleep."

Veraguth closed Pierre's eyes gently and hummed softly to him as he had sometimes done when he was a baby. And the child seemed to fall asleep.

An hour later the nurse came in to call Veraguth to table and relieve him at Pierre's bedside. He went to the dining room, silently and absently ate a dish of soup, scarcely hearing what was said around him. The child's tender, frightened, loving whispers echoed sweet and sad in his ears. Oh, how many hundreds of times he might have talked with Pierre like that, savoring the naïve trust of his carefree love, and had neglected to do so.

(201

Mechanically he reached for the carafe to pour himself water. And then his dream was shattered by a piercing scream from Pierre's room. All three jumped up with pale faces, the carafe was overturned, rolled over the table, and fell to the floor.

In an instant Veraguth was out the door and in Pierre's room.

"The ice bag!" cried the nurse.

He heard nothing. Nothing but that terrible, desperate scream which stuck in his consciousness as a knife in a wound. He rushed to the bed.

There lay Pierre as white as snow, his mouth hideously distorted; his emaciated limbs writhed in furious convulsions, his eyes stared in unreasoning horror. And suddenly he uttered another scream, wilder and louder than the last, and his body arched up so violently that the bedstead trembled; and then it slumped and rose up again, tense with pain and bent like a switch in the hands of an angry boy.

All stood helpless with horror, until the nurse's commands created order. Veraguth kneeled down by the bed and tried to prevent Pierre from hurting himself in his convulsions. Even so, the child's right hand struck itself bloody on the metal rim of the bed. Then he slumped, turned over on his stomach, bit silently into the pillow, and began to kick his left leg rhythmically. He lifted it, brought it down with a stamping move-

ment, rested a moment, and then made the same move-
ment again, ten times, twenty times, and on and on.

The women were at work making compresses, Albert
had been sent away. Veraguth was still on his knees,
looking on as the child's leg rose with uncanny regu-
larity under the blanket, stretched out, and fell. There
lay his child, whose smile only a few hours ago had
been like sunshine and whose imploring, loving bab-
bling had touched and enchanted his heart to its deepest depths. There he lay and was nothing more than a
mechanically quivering body, a poor helpless bundle of
pain and misery.

"We're here with you," he cried in despair. "Pierre,
child, we're here and trying to help you."

But the path from his lips to the child's mind was cut
off, his imploring words of comfort, his tender meaningless whisperings no longer penetrated the terrible
loneliness of the dying child. He was far away in
another world, wandering thirst-parched through a hell
of torment and death, and there perhaps, in the valley
of hell, was crying out for the very man who was
kneeling by his side, who would gladly have suffered
every torment to help his child.

They all knew that this was the end. Since that first
terrifying scream so full of deep animal suffering,
death had lurked in every window and doorway of the
house. No one spoke of it, but all had recognized it,

Albert, too, and the maids downstairs and even the dog, who ran around restlessly on the gravel walk, now and then letting out a frightened whimper. And though they all did what they could, boiled water, brought ice, and kept very busy, the fight was over, the hope had gone out of it.

Pierre had lost consciousness. His whole body trembled as with cold, occasionally he uttered a feeble delirious scream, and time and time again, after a pause of exhaustion, his leg began to kick and to stamp, rhythmically as though moved by clockwork.

So the afternoon passed and the evening and finally the night. It was not until morning, when the little fighter had exhausted his strength and surrendered to the enemy, that the parents exchanged a silent glance out of sleepless eyes. Johann Veraguth laid his hand on Pierre's heart and felt no beat, and he left his hand on the child's sunken chest until it grew cool and cold.

Then he gently stroked Frau Adele's folded hands and said in a whisper: "It's all over." As he led his wife from the room, supporting her and listening to her hoarse sobbing; as he entrusted her to the nurse and listened at Albert's door to see whether he was awake; as he went back to Pierre and straightened him out in his bed, he felt that half his life had died away and been laid to rest.

With composure he did what was necessary. Then at

length he left the dead child to the nurse, and lay down to a short, deep sleep. When the full daylight shone through the windows, he awoke, arose at once, and set about the last piece of work he meant to do at Rosshalde. He went to Pierre's room and opened all the curtains, letting the cool autumnal light shine on his darling's little white face and stiff hands. Then he sat down near the bed, spread out a sheet of paper, and for the last time drew the features which he had studied so often, which he had known and loved since their tender beginnings, and which were now matured and simplified by death, but still full of ununderstood suffering.

Chapter Eighteen

THE SUN WAS SHINING fiery-red through the fringes of the limp, rained-out clouds as the little family rode home from Pierre's funeral. Frau Adele sat erect in the carriage; her face, drained with weeping, seemed strangely bright and rigid as it looked out from between her black hat and her black, high-cut dress. Albert's eyelids were swollen and throughout the ride he held his mother's hand.

"So you'll be leaving tomorrow," said Veraguth in an effort to distract them. "Don't worry about a thing, I'll attend to everything that has to be done. Chin up, my boy."

At Rosshalde, as they descended from the carriage, the dripping branches of the chestnut trees glittered in the light. Dazzled, they entered the silent house, where the maids, clothed in mourning, had been whispering as they waited. Veraguth had locked up Pierre's room.

Coffee was ready and the three sat down to table.

"I've taken rooms for you in Montreux," said Veraguth. "See that you get a good rest. I shall be leaving too, as soon as I've finished here. Robert will stay and keep the house in order. He will have my address."

No one was listening to him; a profound, shaming emptiness weighed on them all like a frost. Frau Adele looked fixedly into space and gathered crumbs from the tablecloth. She shut herself up in her grief, unwilling to be roused, and Albert imitated her. Now that little Pierre lay dead, all semblance of unity in the family had vanished, just as the politeness maintained by an effort of the will vanishes from a man's face as soon as a feared and powerful guest has gone away. Veraguth alone rose above the circumstances, playing his role and preserving his mask to the last moment. He feared that a womanish scene might mar his leave-taking from Rosshalde, and in his heart he waited fervently for the moment when the two of them would be gone.

Never had he been so alone as sitting in his little room that evening. Over in the manor house, his wife was packing. He had written letters, to Burkhardt, who had not yet been told of Pierre's death, announcing his arrival; to his lawyer and bank, giving them their final instructions. Then, when his desk had been cleared, he propped up his drawing of the dead Pierre before him. Now he was lying in the ground, and Veraguth wondered if he would ever again be able to give his heart to anyone as he had to Pierre, ever again share so deeply in anyone else's suffering. Now he was alone.

For a long while he looked at his drawing, the slack cheeks, the lids closed over sunken eyes, the thin, pressed lips, the cruelly emaciated hands. Then he locked up his drawing in the studio, took his coat, and went out. It was already night in the park and everything was still. Over in the house, a few windows were lighted; they did not concern him. But under the black chestnut trees, in the rain-drenched little arbor on the gravel walk, and in the flower garden, there was still a breath of life and memory. Here Pierre had once—had it not been years ago?—showed him a little captive mouse, and over there by the phlox he had spoken with the swarms of blue butterflies, and he had invented tender fanciful names for the flowers. Here, between henhouse and kennel, on the lawn and on the walk under the lime trees, he had led his little life and played his games; here his light, free, boyish laughter and all the charm of his self-willed, independent nature had been at home. Here, observed by no one, he had enjoyed his childlike pleasures and lived his fairy tales, and sometimes perhaps he had been angry or wept when he felt neglected or misunderstood.

Veraguth wandered about in the darkness, visiting every spot that preserved a memory of his little boy. Last he knelt down by Pierre's sand pile and cooled his hands in the damp sand. His hands encountered something wooden and, picking it up, he recognized Pierre's sand shovel. And then he broke down, his will abandoned him, and for the first time in those three terrible days, he was able to weep without restraint.

The next day he had a last talk with Frau Adele.

"Try to get over it," he said, "and don't forget that Pierre belongs to me. You would have given him up to me, and I thank you again for that. Even then I knew he was going to die, but it was generous of you. And now live exactly as you please, and don't be in a hurry about anything. Keep Rosshalde for the present, you might regret it if you sold it too soon. The notary will keep you informed, he says the price of land around here is sure to go up. I wish you the best of luck. There's nothing left here that belongs to me except the things in the studio, I shall have them taken away later on."

"Thank you . . . And you? You'll never come here any more?"

"No. There would be no point. And I wanted to tell you this: I feel no more bitterness. I know that I myself was to blame for everything."

"Don't say that. You mean well, but it only makes me miserable. And now you're staying behind all by yourself. It wouldn't be so bad if you had been able to keep Pierre. But as it is—no, this shouldn't have happened. I've been to blame too, I know . . ."

"We've made atonement these last few days. You

mustn't fret, everything will be all right, there's really nothing to have regrets about. Look, now you have Albert all to yourself. And I, I have my work. That makes everything bearable. And you too will be happier than you've been for years."

He was so calm that she too controlled herself. Oh, there were many things, very many, that she would have liked to say, things she would have liked to thank him for, or hold up to him. But she saw that he was right. It was plain that to him everything that she still felt to be life and bitterly present had already become shadowy past. There was nothing else to do but be calm and let the past be past. And so she listened patiently and attentively to his instructions, surprised at how thoroughly he had thought it all out.

Not a word was said of divorce. That could be taken care of some time in the future when he returned from India.

After lunch they drove to the station. There stood Robert with all the suitcases, and amid the noise and soot of the great glass dome Veraguth saw the two of them into the carriage, bought magazines for Albert, gave him the baggage check, and waited outside the window until the train moved off. Then he took off his hat and waved it and looked after the train until Albert disappeared from the window.

On the way home, Robert, in response to his inquiry,

told him how he had broken off his overhasty engagement. At the house the carpenter was waiting to crate Veraguth's last paintings. Once they were packed and sent away, he too would leave. He longed to be gone.

And now the carpenter had finished his work. Robert was working at the manor house with one maid who had stayed on; they covered the furniture and locked the doors and windows.

Veraguth strode slowly through his studio, then through his living room and bedroom. Then he went out, around the lake and through the park. He had taken this walk a hundred times, but today everything, house and garden, lake and park, seemed to echo loneliness. The wind blew cold in the yellowing leaves and brought new fleecy rain clouds in low-hovering files. The painter shivered with the cold. Now they were all gone. There was no one here to care for, to be considerate of, no one in whose presence he had to maintain his composure, and only now, in this frozen loneliness, were the cares and sleepless nights, the quivering fever and all the crushing weariness borne in on him. He felt them not only in his mind and bones but deep in his heart. In those days the last shimmering lights of youth and expectancy had been extinguished; but the cold isolation and cruel disenchantment no longer frightened him.

Sauntering on along the wet paths, he tried to follow

back the threads of his life, whose simple fabric he had never before seen so clearly. It came to him without bitterness that he had followed all those pathways blindly. He saw clearly that despite his many attempts, despite the yearning that had never left him, he had passed the garden of life by. Never had he lived out a love to its bottommost depths, never until these last days. At the bedside of his dying child he had known, all too late, his only true love; then he had forgotten, and risen above, himself. And now that would be his experience, his poor little treasure, as long as he lived.

What remained to him was his art, of which he had never felt as sure as he did now. There remained the consolation of the outsider, to whom it is not given to seize the cup of life and drain it; there remained the strange, cool, and yet irresistible passion to see, to observe, and to participate with secret pride in the work of creation. That was the residue and the value of his unsuccessful life, the imperturbable loneliness and cold delight of art, and to follow that star without detours would from now on be his destiny.

He breathed deeply the moist, bitter-scented air of the park and at every step it seemed to him that he was pushing away the past as one who has reached the shore pushes away a skiff, now useless. His probing and his insight were without resignation; full of defiance and venturesome passion, he looked forward to the new life, which, he was resolved, would no longer be a groping or dim-sighted wandering but rather a bold, steep climb. Later and more painfully perhaps than most men, he had taken leave of the sweet twilight of youth. Now he stood poor and belated in the broad daylight, and of that he meant never again to lose a precious hour.